Enchanted
Runner

Enchanted Runner

Kimberley Griffiths Little

AN AVON CAMELOT BOOK

AVON BOOKS, INC.
1350 Avenue of the Americas
New York, New York 10019

Copyright © 1999 by Kimberley Griffiths Little
Interior design by Kellan Peck
ISBN: 0-380-97623-4

Library of Congress Cataloging in Publication Data:
Little, Kimberley Griffiths.
    Enchanted runner / Kimberley Griffiths Little. —1st ed.
    p. cm.
    Summary: Twelve-year-old Kendall, half Anglo and half Acoma, discovers his heritage and his destiny as a runner when he visits his great-grandfather's pueblo and finds a culture he used to hear about from his deceased mother.
    1. Acoma Indians—Juvenile fiction. [1. Acoma Indians—Fiction. 2. Indians of North America—New Mexico—Fiction. 3. Racially mixed people—Fiction. 4. Great-grandfathers—Fiction. 5. Running—Fiction. 6. Acoma (N.M.)—Fiction.] I. Title.
PZ7.L72256En 1999   98-54849
[Fic]—dc21   CIP
                                                                                 AC

First Avon Camelot Printing: August 1999

CAMELOT TRADEMARK REG. U.S. PAT. OFF. AND IN OTHER COUNTRIES, MARCA REGISTRADA, HECHO EN U.S.A.

Printed in the U.S.A.

FIRST EDITION

QPM 10 9 8 7 6 5 4 3 2 1

www.avonbooks.com

This book is for Carmel Keyope and her three sons, Jonathan, David, and Michael, with love and gratitude for sharing the dances, stories, and traditions of Acoma. My heart is full of admiration for their heritage, faith, and generosity. I cherish the time I've spent with them and being a part of their lives.

ACKNOWLEDGMENTS

I want to express love and thanks to some special people who gave me wonderful feedback and advice during the creation of this book: Cindy-Rae Jones, Sheila Wood Foard, Kristin Litchman, Linda Herman, and as always, my dearest husband, Rusty. Great appreciation also goes to my wonderful agent, Irene Kraas, and terrific editor, Abigail McAden, for their enthusiasm and guidance.

Kendall knew magic existed in the universe. He could feel it whenever he ran—an invisible power that swirled in the air, luring him like the chocolate fudge cake his mother used to have waiting for him on the kitchen table after school.

The forces of magic pulled so strongly, Kendall finally gave up walking. He ran everywhere. Each day he jogged the halls between classrooms, then sprinted home after school.

And every afternoon that unseen power wrapped itself around Kendall's feet during the sixth-grade races. He zoomed over the blacktop, passing all the other kids in a blur of shorts and sneakers until he was alone. Just him and the magic.

Sometimes he'd close his eyes and try to grab it, but it always stayed just out of reach, elusive and tantalizing.

When Mr. Crawford blasted the whistle, Kendall braked too hard on his Nikes and nearly fell on the asphalt. Swiping at his hot face with the tail of his T-shirt, he looked over his shoulder, and his heart sank. The hundred-yard dash had ended two hundred feet behind him.

The rest of the class laughed and a couple of kids pointed at him. "There goes the running maniac," someone said across the blacktop. "Doesn't know when to stop," another voice added. There were more giggles.

Kendall had been called a running maniac all year. He never seemed to see the finish line and he never stopped, even when the race was over. He couldn't explain it. Something pushed him forward, an enchantment that sped up his feet even when he crossed the finish line.

At times he could have sworn he was running faster than any world-champion runner ever had. As fast as a wild horse galloped. It was weird. Where did this strange enchantment come from? Why had it gotten even stronger now that Mom was gone?

A hot breeze lifted his hair and Kendall could see a horse in his mind, a beautiful shimmering dream horse running over the desert. And he was next to it. The image reminded him of the stories Mom used to tell him late at night when he couldn't sleep. A story about warriors from Mom's native tribe crossing the desert on their horses, coming home to the cliffs of Acoma. But the stories were just dreams. Kendall had never ridden a horse in his life, and he hadn't ever seen Acoma, except in his dreams.

But a wild horse was fast, and wild horses didn't have to stop at finish lines.

"Okay, kids, last round," Mr. Crawford called. "The final bell's about to ring."

The next heat lined up and Kendall took a spot at the end. Mr. Crawford blew the whistle for the race to begin just as the three o'clock bell rang. The last bell of the school year.

The lineup of racers fell apart as kids hollered for joy and streamed across the playground, heading for the yellow buses.

Only Kendall took off, pulled by the mysterious, magical cord.

"Hey, Drennan! You can stop now," the teacher cried. "Everybody is gone. There's no one to race."

Kendall turned in his tracks and grinned, running backward into the field and hoping he didn't fall into a tumbleweed. "I don't need anybody to run against," he yelled, the power of the magic making him talk crazy.

The hot May sun burned through his shirt as Kendall rounded the school buildings and headed for the road that led home. There weren't any sidewalks, just a dirt shoulder off the uneven asphalt. He jumped through ragweed and piles of old cottonwood leaves.

It was a good day. The last day of school always was.

On Monday he and Dad and Brett were going to leave in the eighteen-wheel semi-truck for the whole summer. His brother Brett, who was seventeen, had gone on long hauls during past summers. This year Kendall got to go with them. Just the three of them in the rig, far away for months, stopping at truck stops, going to Disneyland.

Kendall poured on the speed, cutting over to the ditch bank. The muddy Rio Grande rippled behind giant cottonwood trees.

He crossed the ditch along a homemade plank bridge, passing scattered houses and a dairy farm. After a stretch of corn and alfalfa fields, he made the turn onto his own narrow, dusty road.

Kendall tore down the slope of the trailer park, gravel flying with each step, magic pouring over him like a waterfall. He swiped at his face and mouth, tasting fresh sweat.

Crashing into the chain-link fence, Kendall felt his legs tremble. He leaned over, gasping in great gulps of air, as the magic melted away. He'd never made the connection, no matter how fast and hard he ran—never managed to grasp the cords that tugged at him every day.

Kendall tried to steady himself, overwhelmed by the power of it all. Nobody saw how much he ran. Hundred-yard dashes at school were nothing. His real running had become a secret too big to explain, too important to share.

Last year, the sicker Mom got, the faster Kendall ran home from school. He began timing himself the minute the three o'clock bell rang. When he burst in the front door, Mom was always dressed and reading a book in the rocking chair, waiting for him even if she was very tired.

"You're getting to be quite the track star," she had said one day. When Kendall drew closer, she told him, "My father ran when he was young. For a special ceremony at Old Acoma."

Kendall wanted her to tell him more, but she shook her head, tears filling her eyes. The sicker she became, the harder it was for her to talk about Acoma and her memories. All she said was "Whenever you run, Kendall, run with everything inside your heart."

As Kendall gripped the fence, an image of waist-length black hair clouded his mind. Memories of his mother made him dizzy.

Right before she died, the household became crazy with nurses and people bringing in food. Kendall tried to tell Mom about the magical waves that pulled him across the ground until he felt like he was flying. He was sure his mother could explain the feelings he had, but she was pulled away by the home-care nurse for shots and medicine. The living room had become like a hospital, with his mother in a bed that moved up and down by remote control.

She made an effort to raise her head from the pillow. "There is a place, my son," she whispered as the nurse prepared the needle. "A place that has all the answers." It was clear she hadn't understood him.

By then, chances to talk to her alone were rare. And that opportunity turned out to be his last.

Kendall slammed the fence with both fists and looked up, the bright sun making his eyes water. Heat steamed off the gleaming red semi in the driveway. Dad was home.

The hood of the truck was propped up and Brett's tall, lanky figure appeared through the shed doors in the backyard. He held a wrench in his greasy hands and raised it at the sight of Kendall. "Hey, kid, you better start packing. We're leaving first thing Monday."

"Yahoo!" Kendall cried. The excitement of the trip had been building for weeks. They were leaving, and they weren't coming back until August.

"Make sure you got plenty of underwear," Brett told him, and laughed. "You know, we're not even stopping to do laundry."

"Yeah, right," Kendall said.

"Hey, if you don't believe me, ask Dad."

"Get out of here."

Brett's blond head disappeared under the truck's hood. A moment later he jumped inside the cab and revved the motor. Brett loved trucks as much as Dad did. They looked alike and had similar interests: trucks and softball games and fast food. Since Mom died, they had become inseparable. Brett was nearly a man, and it showed in how he and Dad treated each other and talked together. But after a cross-country summer in the truck, Kendall hoped he would become one of them and would not be considered a little kid anymore.

Clanging the gate, Kendall turned on the hose at the outside faucet. He stuck his thumb on the end and held the hose over his head, yelping when the icy spray hit his sweaty body.

Voices in the neighbor's yard made Kendall glance over. Matthew, who was in kindergarten, was swinging in the inner tube hanging from their cottonwood tree. His mom was pushing him and they were giggling about something.

He threw the hose down on the porch and brushed his arm against his eyes, unable to look at them. He was jealous of a six-year-old. That was dumb. By the time you were twelve, boys weren't supposed to want their mothers.

A cold trickle crept down Kendall's neck when he stepped inside the front door. The swamp cooler was running. He could smell the mustiness. Dad wasn't in the living room, but Kendall couldn't even see the couch, it was so littered with sections of newspapers and magazines. Every month a new layer of junk was added to the piles of dust.

In the kitchen, paper plates stood stacked in a big heap, chunks of dried food stuck to them. The counters held several days worth of Taco Bell bags and flattened hot sauce packets. Melted ice laced with flat Dr Pepper settled at the bottom of old paper cups.

Kendall was getting sick of Taco Bell.

Egg McMuffins for breakfast, cafeteria for lunch, and Taco Bell for dinner. Kendall couldn't remember the last time they'd gone to Kentucky Fried Chicken or Wendy's. Dad was stuck in a rut.

What did Mom used to fix? Kendall thought back to nights of homemade rolls and green chili stew. Fry bread and honey. Mounds of mashed potatoes he used to form into a castle with a moat for the gravy. All those things plus more, but it was fading.

For months he clung to old memories. Before he went to sleep, he could bring up her face, like a computer game, but now even that had begun to blur. He could still hear her voice, but he was afraid that one day that would also be gone.

Now, almost a year later, Kendall still ran. At first he ran to save her. Now he ran to get the memory of her face back. That wasn't too much to ask, was it? But sometimes he felt frantic. It didn't seem to make any difference. He was losing her. And yet the magic lured him, never letting him go.

Kendall rubbed a hand across his mouth. There had to be another reason the enchantment pestered him, another reason he ran, but he hadn't figured it out yet. It was like something coming up and tapping him on the shoulder, and yet no matter how fast he whirled around, he could never catch it in the act.

Dad was seated at the kitchen table, stacks of bills and junk mail spread all over. His head rested on his knuckles and his palms dug into his eyes.

On one end of the table, an atlas and a stack of maps lay in disarray. Kendall had marked the route for freight pick-ups in green and deliveries in red. He'd figured out the mileage and the places they'd stop along the way.

Kendall stepped closer and his father jumped. Dad wiped his eyes and sniffed; then he grinned and pulled Kendall onto a chair next to him. "You caught me again."

The photo albums were open, albums stuffed full of pictures from the first years of his parents' marriage. Dad spent a lot of hours with them.

Kendell glanced at the snapshots of his parents' college days, their wedding at a friend's house, his mother receiving her diploma, but these photos were not how he remembered her. Sometimes Kendall felt as if he had nothing of her. He'd been cheated in a game where the rules changed every time he turned around.

Dad picked up a piece of paper, crumpled around the edges where his fingers gripped it. "I got this today."

Anxiety began to grow in Kendall's stomach. "What is it?"

"A letter."

His father paused so long, Kendall felt the urge to say something obnoxious, but then he noticed the tears welling up in Dad's eyes. He had never seen any other man cry. But Dad often did. Dad cried so much that Kendall couldn't.

"My own mama said I was a crybaby as a boy, and I turned into a bawling grown-up." Dad tried to smile and cleared his throat. "The letter is from your great-grandfather."

"But he died a long time ago."

"Not my family, son. I'm talking about your mother's family. The Abeytas."

Kendall studied his father's face, the light blue eyes and the freckles that he hadn't inherited. His own skin was golden brown, as if he'd spent a lot of time in the sun, but not quite as dark as his mother's had been. It was funny how he could suddenly see her arms, the turquoise and silver bracelets and rings she wore to work, her wedding band, but nothing else. He blinked and the picture disappeared. He tried so hard not to blink, but in the end his eyes always betrayed him.

"Where do they live?" Kendall finally asked.

"Acoma. They call it Sky City."

He knew that. Kendall didn't know why he'd asked. His mother had often told him about her homeland; small things, as if they were reminiscing about someplace they both already knew. But Kendall couldn't have told anyone else what the pueblo was like, only the descriptions in his mind that his mother had put there. She had never taken him.

"I don't get it," Kendall said. His stomach squeezed tightly.

"When she married me—" His father's voice cracked, and his eyes were so full of tears, Kendall wondered how he could keep them from falling.

"Was her grandfather mad? Did she ever go back?" Kendall knew what had happened, but he'd never heard it from his father's lips. Only his mother's story, told in her Indian version when she tucked him in at night.

"I'm sure he was angry. Definitely he felt hurt and betrayed. Rebecca married an Anglo. She was supposed to be the clan matriarch, the last of the Rattlesnakes or something."

"Snake Clan," Kendall whispered.

His father looked up, surprised. "That's right. How did you remember that?"

Kendall shrugged, embarrassed to tell his father how often he heard his mother's voice in his head. "Good memory, I guess."

Dad smiled. "Guess so. You're a smart kid. I'm gonna—"

There was that twist in the gut again.

His father spread the letter on the table, but Kendall couldn't look at it. He sat locked in his seat, damp jeans and sweaty T-shirt stuck to his skin. Waiting for his father to get to the important part.

"She only went back once. Seventeen years ago when she took Brett as a baby." Dad's voice broke and he put his head in his hands again. "I feel guilty. Like I stole her or something. And now she's gone forever."

Kendall watched the tears finally overflow, trickling to his father's chin.

"Last summer when I had to write the old man," he said softly, "it was the hardest thing I ever did. He never acknowledged it. Armando Abeyta's gotta be pushing a hundred—born around the turn of the century, I think. I wasn't even sure he was still alive. But Rebecca wrote to

9

them every Christmas." Dad added, "And years ago she made a promise."

Kendall knew what the promise was.

"When you were twelve she was going to take you to Acoma."

Dad stopped and Kendall raised his face. Their eyes met.

"Your great-grandmother died a few weeks ago. It took him a while to write, probably had to think things out. But it looks like he wants me to keep the promise. He wants you, buddy."

2

Kendall punched his pillow. It was late, had to be past midnight, and his throat felt so constricted he could hardly swallow.

He tried to capture his mother's face, but her image was slippery, like a wet glass crashing to the floor through his fingers. It wasn't fair. He shouldn't have to do this alone—without her, without Dad.

But Dad had signed cross-country contracts for the summer. He couldn't back out. He drove locally during the school year, but the cross-country hauls paid better, and the three of them decided to spend their first summer without Mom in the truck together. Used to be Mom was home, off from her teaching position at the high school. There would be trips to the ice-cream parlor for banana splits and swimming at the local pool, staying up late to watch videos. Sometimes they sat outside to watch the moon rise and Mom would write letters or poetry, her long hair draped over her arm. Kendall felt like he'd been robbed.

Then last night there was the argument.

After dinner, Dad had casually said to Brett, "Maybe I

should send you with Kendall. I'm sure your great-grandfather wouldn't mind. He only saw you once when you were just a baby. It was the first time your mother went to visit after we were married. The last time, too," Dad added sadly. "I think I'll write to him. Or maybe I better telephone."

Then the shouting started. It made Kendall's stomach hurt to listen to them.

"Are you crazy?" Brett had yelled. "No way am I going to spend my summer at some Indian reservation."

"How about Kendall? I'll know you'll be there to watch out for him. Brett, this is your great-grandfather we're talking about," Dad had said halfheartedly.

"Since when has he ever cared? We've never even met him."

"Don't you care about your mother?" Dad finally exploded.

That shut Brett up for a minute. In a quieter voice, he said, "Sure I care about Mom. But I don't know anything about her Indian stuff. Remember, Dad, I wasn't even invited. Send Kendall. He'll be okay. And that'll ease the old man's guilt."

"Don't be disrespectful," Dad had cut in sharply.

"I'm sorry, it's just that it's awfully funny all of a sudden, now that Mom's gone, he wants to meet Kendall."

Dad fell wearily onto a kitchen chair. "I admit I don't want to be alone myself all summer," he said to Brett. "I may need your help with repairs or flat tires."

Kendall had tried to speak, but the two tall males in front of him in the kitchen were too much. Finally he blurted, "Why do I have to go? This is my first long trip in the truck. That's not fair."

"We can sacrifice the kid, can't we?" Brett said, ruffling Kendall's hair.

Kendall hit his brother's hand away. "Cut it out."

"Nobody is getting sacrificed," Dad said.

"I don't want to be alone either," Kendall said. "Please don't make me, Dad. Please."

"You won't be alone, buddy. You'll be with your great-grandfather and his family. You'll get to see where Mom grew up and all the places she always told you about."

"You feel guilty, too," Brett told his father as he opened the refrigerator.

Kendall was always amazed at the way his older brother talked to their father, as if they were both equals. He got away with it because they were so close and so much alike. Kendall felt as if he were the odd one out.

"I probably am," Dad admitted, sighing. "But Armando Abeyta is trying to make some kind of amends here and we can't just throw it in his face. He raised your mother like a daughter, and she never saw him again."

They weren't listening to him and Kendall realized his own arguments weren't working. This couldn't be happening. All of a sudden, what was supposed to be the best summer of his life had been turned upside down, canceled. Just like that.

Kendall wasn't giving up. "Dad, I don't want to go. You promised me I could go in the truck this year."

Dad turned away, jaw tight. "Let's talk about it later." He banged the kitchen screen door and disappeared outside.

Later, his father moped around the house and ended up falling asleep in front of the TV.

Kendall woke him to file an official protest. "I'm not going," he announced when Dad turned off the television. "It's not fair, and you can't make me."

"Oh, son," Dad said sadly. He gestured for Kendall to come closer.

Kendall moved stiffly across the room and his father

pulled him down on the couch next to him. "I want you to see something."

Reid Drennan reached over to the coffee table and pulled open a book. It was Mom's journal. "I've read this several times since your mother passed away. It gives me some comfort. When you're a grown man, maybe I'll let you read the whole book, but right now I think you need to see something. In fact, it's one of the last things she wrote."

His mother's perfect handwriting flowed across the crisp white pages. Kendall found it hard to breathe as he read about her secret dream to return to Acoma and take Kendall with her.

Kendall has so many parts of Acoma inside him. It shows in his face, and in the way he listens to my stories. My book of Acoma stories will have to wait until another life to finish writing them. It looks as if my longing to go back to Acoma will happen only in my dreams. The urgency I feel increases the closer I get to death. I hope the gods do not prevent my spirit from returning when I pass through the doorway.

Kendall lay stiff on his bed and watched the shadows move across his wall. His duffel bag was half packed. Clothes spilled all over his room from the last load in the dryer, needing to be folded and stuffed into the duffel. Kendall couldn't sleep with all the stuff whirling around in his brain.

Tomorrow Dad was going to try to call the pueblo and speak to Armando Abeyta and confirm their plans. His great-grandfather hadn't specified any day, just wanted him to come and spend part of the summer. Dad promised it would only be for a few weeks. Then he and Brett would pick Kendall up in July and still go to Disneyland or someplace for a real vacation.

After Dad showed him his mother's journal, Kendall knew he had to go. Dad wasn't letting him back out for a second. But ever since Kendall had read Mom's words, a new thought wrestled in his brain. Maybe his mother was at Acoma. What if she had been secretly hiding there all this time, waiting for him? The thought made the hair on the back of his neck rise.

Kendall rolled over. His mother hadn't had a chance to prepare him for her grandfather's house. What was it like? How should he act? Would he be welcome?

"When you're twelve, we will go to Acoma," she had said once a long time ago. "It will be the right time to show you Sky City, and time to fix the past. You are like him— my grandfather, the father who raised me."

How could he be like someone he'd never met? When Mom talked about going, it was far in the future, and they would have been together. He hadn't worried about it.

Now the letter had come, changing the summer.

This was the summer he was twelve. Twelve and three months, and his mother always kept her promises.

The rig's engine was rumbling in the driveway when Kendall woke up on Monday morning. He tossed his pajamas in his duffel bag, yanked on his jeans, and looked out the window.

There it was. Ten tons of shining silver, a gleaming red cab, the exhaust pipe belching smoke three feet into the sky. Dad straightened up from the open engine, slammed the huge domed hood shut, then stashed his toolbox inside the cab.

Kendall loved the sound that the eighteen-wheeler made. He was going to ride with Dad west on Highway 40 about sixty miles until they took the road south to Sky City.

Dad had contracted for several pickups along the coast

between L.A. and Seattle. Kendall was also going to miss going through Wyoming all the way to Chicago. After that, Dad had some hauling to do between New York and Denver. But Dad promised he'd pick Kendall up for his last round between California and Florida before school started.

Almost two months without seeing his dad. Kendall already felt homesick. Homesick for the smell of the truck and keeping track of the log and the gas mileage. Helping fill the tank at the truck stops. Paying for the big drinks at the soda fountain. Popping in the CDs as Dad drove.

"I owe him," Dad kept repeating all weekend. "I'm sorry to do this to you, buddy."

"It's not your fault Mom died," Brett told him.

"Is he going to be in a wheelchair or something?" Kendall asked, fearing the worst. Cooped up in some ratty house with a sick old man who was blind or needed hearing aids.

"Have no idea, but he wrote the letter himself. Good penmanship, so we know his hands still work."

Kendall watched Dad smile at him, but the gnawing, anxious feeling grew stronger.

"What do I do? Can he speak English?" Kendall had asked as they sat inside the air-conditioned Taco Bell Saturday night.

Dad laughed at that, and Kendall realized it was a stupid question.

"Unless I learned Keresan in my sleep," Dad said. "I could read his letter."

"She always called him father, but wasn't he really her grandfather?" Kendall asked. "What happened? I can't remember."

"Your mother never knew her actual parents. Her father was killed in combat during the Korean War soon after they were married. Then your grandmother died giving birth to your mother. I think it was toxemia or something. There wasn't a hospital back then and conditions were poverty level. In many ways, they still are."

"That's sad to have both your parents die."

"I'm sure it was terrible for Armando and his wife, Lydia, but your mother was a baby and didn't know any differently. She loved her grandparents as her own parents. I know she would love to be with you now going to Acoma," Dad added.

"Mom should be taking me—she *promised*." Kendall never said things like that about his mother, but this time he couldn't help it.

Dad put down his burrito and nodded. "I know, buddy, I know. But the sickness within her own body never promised her a long life."

"She told me she was going to Si-pa-pu when she died," Kendall said. "The place where the people first came from. Do you think she's really there?"

Brett rolled his eyes, but Dad looked up from his dinner. His father always took his questions seriously. "Well, son, I'm not sure if she's in Si-pa-pu. Don't know much about that. But I believe she still exists somewhere, even though we can't see her or be with her. I don't think she's completely gone. Mostly because I can still feel her."

It was exactly what Kendall thought. And what he hoped to find by going to Acoma. He zipped his duffel bag and threw the sheets over his pillow in an attempt to make the bed. Then he closed the window, muting the sound the semi generated, and wondered if Mrs. Weigart across the street would call about the noise.

Kendall glanced back at his bedroom, suddenly not wanting to leave it. Just a few days ago he wouldn't have cared, he was so anxious to get on the road with Dad, but now everything was different.

Brett was up early and packing the truck. Kendall watched him through the window as he ate a bowl of cold cereal, then brushed his teeth.

Dad came in the back door to wash his grease-stained hands. "Gotta get moving. I want to make Kingman by tonight. My pickup is at three tomorrow afternoon in L.A."

Kendall followed his father into the master bedroom, where Dad picked up his own duffel bag and shaving kit, then checked the window locks.

"I think we're ready to go," Dad said, bumping his bag down the hall. "Everything else is in the truck."

"Okay, I'll be right out." Kendall hesitated, listened to the back door slam, then returned to his father's bedroom. There was something he had to get.

He opened the closet and fingered his mother's skirts and blouses. Dad hadn't given them away yet. Her bureau drawers were also untouched. Dad said he would go through her belongings at the end of the summer, when it had been a year.

Kendall opened the top dresser drawer, slipped his hand under the sweaters, and grabbed what he was after. Mom had given the Native American relic to him when he was eight. When she died, he put it back with her belongings, to absorb her memories.

So far it hadn't worked. Dad didn't even know it was there inside the drawer. But Kendall couldn't leave it. What if somebody robbed their house while they were gone? That probably wouldn't happen, though, since Dad had hired Jake, the high school boy down the street, to watch their place and bring in the mail.

Kendall closed his palm around the slim handmade circle and quickly stuffed it inside his shirt so it wouldn't get crushed. This had to go with him to Acoma. Back where it came from. Perhaps it would work there.

3

Kendall crammed his bag into the sleeper section of the cab. Dad's and Brett's stuff was already there, along with the photo albums of Mom and the mini television hooked on to the wall over the foot of the bed.

The truck's idle vibrated so strongly it shook the cab as Kendall fastened his seat belt. He blinked hard. Tears pricked his eyes, blurring the trailer and the weedy front yard.

He watched Dad shift into gear and back out of the driveway. Dad took the Highway 6 shortcut, a two-lane road through rolling desert covered with wild grasses. They passed a few trailers plopped at funny angles far off the road, shabby barns and stacks of rubber tires in their yards.

Sitting high in the truck, Kendall watched red canyons and arroyos float by. Deep ravines looked like earthquake cracks. The highway followed the train tracks, and Dad pointed out every train that passed as if Kendall couldn't see it himself.

"Man, you are one crazy kid," Brett said again. He'd been saying it all weekend. "You really want to go? You couldn't pay me enough."

"Brett," Dad warned.

"Just shut up," Kendall told his brother.

"Can't we get along for two hours?" Dad asked. "What would we do if we were going to be together for the entire summer?"

It wasn't that Kendall *wanted* to go. It was more like he *had* to go. For his mother. For himself. For the magic. If Mom was at Acoma, then Brett was going to miss out.

Kendall smiled deep inside. His brother didn't know everything.

They fell into silence and he tried to relax next to Brett, who was keeping time to one of the country CDs.

He shifted in his seat. It was more than nerves or butterflies. More than gnawing anxiety about a new place and new people. This place and these people were his mother's. He wanted to do the right thing, say the right words.

The miles sped by, as if the truck and the whole world had suddenly become a video in fast forward. Kendall wanted to slow everything down, make it last for hours. Make it last all summer.

As Dad slowed to make the turn from Highway 6 to Interstate 40 going west, Kendall had the sudden urge to run. He felt the magic teasing him, the cord dangling out in front of him on that stretch of highway. He felt as if he could keep up with the truck, which was going sixty-five miles an hour. Maybe he could even beat the truck there. Kendall tried to push the feeling down, but his legs ached to jump out of the cab.

Mile after mile, he clamped his hands on his thighs to keep them still. On the other side of Brett, Dad chewed his lower lip and frowned at the road. His father hadn't spoken in a while. Now he hunched over the wheel and glanced at Kendall. "This hour's gone too fast. Here's the exit already."

"Bye-bye, baby brother," Brett said.

Kendall wanted to kick him. His stomach flew into his throat as Dad eased the semi down the exit and turned south.

"There's nothing here," Brett said after a mile.

A skinny two-lane road stretched into the hazy heat. Kendall rolled down his window and stuck his head out.

Dad shut off the air-conditioning and slowed down.

Sagebrush and juniper covered the land and wild grasses ruffled under a silent breeze.

Ignoring the waves of enchantment didn't work. They welled up again. He rested his chin on the window ledge, catching his reflection in the rearview mirror, eyes scrunched against the wind.

All of a sudden, behind his right ear, something moved. Kendall leaned out farther. A herd of horses far off the road galloped across the slopes. Colors of chestnut, gold, and black weaved through stands of dark green juniper.

"Did you see that?" Kendall cried, glancing at Dad, then back at the horses.

"Yeah, pretty, aren't they?" Dad agreed.

Brett whistled. "Look at 'em run."

For a moment the horses seemed suddenly closer, catching up to the truck, climbing a rise. In one fluid motion the herd ran, dipping down the slope until it disappeared into a ravine.

Kendall waited to catch sight of them again, but they didn't appear again. "Where'd they go? Where are the owners?"

"No owners," Dad said. "Those are wild horses and they run in groups. Probably several herds out here on the desert."

Wild horses. Just like in the old movies. But these were Acoma wild horses and Kendall had a picture in his mind of an Indian brave riding bareback into the sunset. Did they still do that?

A few minutes later Dad tapped him on the leg. "You can't miss this. Look at that."

Kendall stared out the front window. He gulped. One single enormous white rock soared out of the desert right in front of them. Sheer, straight walls rose almost perfectly circular, kissing the sky.

"Is that it?" he asked. "Is that Acoma?"

Dad shook his head. "Nope, but I almost forgot about that beauty. It's called Enchanted Mesa."

Brett whistled again, long and low.

The strangest feeling rushed over Kendall; he had to close his eyes. Magical cords wrapped around his body, squeezing him until he gasped.

The road curved and ran parallel to the mesa. Dad slowed the truck and rolled down his own window.

"Dad, stop the truck."

"Huh?" his father grunted. "You want to get out?"

Kendall was already pulling on the door handle. "I *have* to get out."

"Hey, don't jump," Dad said, steering the semi onto the dirt shoulder. "You sick or something?"

"Kid, it's confirmed," Brett said. "You are crazy."

Kendall ignored him, popping the door open and jumping past the running board. Exhaust fumes filled his nose as he darted around the front of the rig. He crossed the road, then tore through the knee-high brush, startling a lizard back under its rock.

He had to run or he'd burst. He felt as if there were a power bigger than himself, a monster who held him in its grip.

The truck's idle quickly faded as he ran over rocks and shrubs, climbing the bottom slope of rubble. Finally he neared the jagged, pearly walls of the rock. "Enchanted Mesa," he whispered to the mountain.

Piercing the blue sky, the summit had to be close to five hundred feet. Kendall followed the base to the west, his sneakers slipping over mounds of sand and stones, boulders and gravel.

He wanted to touch the rock itself, feel its craggy roughness, but the broken shale underfoot was so deep and soft it was hard to get close. Kendall scrambled along the sloping base, but the more he ran, the bigger it seemed to grow. It had to be a mile around the whole thing.

Behind him, Dad called his name. Kendall slowed and looked back. The truck had disappeared when he turned the curve of the mesa.

For the moment, he was alone, just short scrub and wild grass for miles. A hot, clear sky arched over the world. Kendall sat down on a pile of pink rocks. He felt a breeze brush his sweaty forehead, as he sucked in the warm air.

Mom had never mentioned this place and Kendall had never felt the magic draw him this strongly. Why hadn't she told him about Enchanted Mesa? What secrets did it hold?

Kendall picked up a handful of sand and his fingers turned dusty white. The wide-open spaces were full of those mysterious gut-wrenching cords.

He wanted to soak it in, but he knew he had to go back. Dad probably thought he really had turned into a maniac, leaping out of the truck like that.

Kendall finally stood up. And that's when he saw the herd of horses.

4

Kendall didn't move a muscle. He tried not to even blink. The horses hadn't seen him yet. Then, out of the mix of blacks and bays, a perfect white horse pulled away from the group and trotted closer to the mesa. Kendall's heart pounded. It was the most beautiful horse he'd ever seen, but when it saw Kendall, the animal halted in its tracks. The black eyes watched him for a moment in which time seemed to stop.

The horse shook its gorgeous, silky mane. Hooves pranced in place, churning the dust; then the horse wheeled and shot across the desert at full speed. The rest of the herd followed, heading for a distant ridge.

Kendall held himself tight, trying not to fling himself across the desert after them.

"Hey, Kendall, there you are." Dad reached out a hand and gasped. "Didn't know where you took off to so fast. You okay?"

"Sure, Dad." Kendall pointed across the sand. "Did you see that horse?"

"What horse?"

"There was a white horse standing by those piñon trees."

"I guess this old trucker scared her off," Dad said. "Hey, we gotta get back. Brett may take off with the rig."

Kendall glanced back once more. He itched to fly across the tall grass, to follow that white horse. That was the horse he would run with. But now the desert was empty. Only a hawk circled the sun.

They returned to the truck and Dad gunned the semi over the steep shoulder back onto the pavement. Three miles farther on Dad raised a hand. "There it is."

An oblong mesa rose alone from the desert floor. It was longer than Enchanted Mesa, but not quite as tall. The red and purple rock looked like waves frozen hundreds of feet in the air.

"Pretty impressive," Dad said, shaking his head in appreciation.

Kendall couldn't stop staring. It was more than impressive. It was like a fortress or a castle from a dream, part of a world different from the one he knew. Mom's words suddenly tickled in his head. She had always said Acoma survived for centuries before the Spaniards came. A world that had existed since the beginning of time. Old like the earth.

"Have you ever been here before?" Kendall asked. "Did you ever meet Mom's grandfather?"

"When your mom and I planned to marry, she took me to meet both of them. Only once, but I'll never forget. There was a crude dirt road put in a couple of decades before, but she made me climb the cliff trail. There are hand- and foot-holds in a crevice of the rock. They used to carry everything up on foot. Food, water, the works. No plumbing or electricity. I think most of the village lives out in Acomita now, in regular homes with bathrooms and stoves and refrigerators."

"Where's the town?" Kendall asked. "Where's Acoma?"

"On top of that mesa, almost four hundred feet in the air," Dad replied. "That's why it's called Sky City. Practically sitting in the clouds."

"But I don't see it," Kendall protested.

Dad chuckled. "Look real close. It's there, all right."

Kendall stared out the windshield. Suddenly, two- and three-story brown adobes linked like apartments came into focus. "The pueblo blends right into the rock," he said.

"Amazing, huh?" Dad said.

"How could they build a town way up there like that?" Brett asked.

"Carried it all up the face of the cliff, if I remember right," Dad told him.

Kendall sat on the edge of his seat. An entire little city with dozens of homes spread across its flat top. He could see the small square chinks for windows and the homemade ladders that led from one roof's level to the next.

"We gotta find a place for this thing," Dad said, trying to maneuver his way into the parking lot.

"Hey, I'll park it for you," Brett offered, but Dad shook his head.

"I'll let you pull out later," Dad told him.

Kendall was jolted to see people and cars milling around a single-story building landscaped with sidewalks and posted signs.

"This is the visitor's center," Dad said, sliding the truck along the back of the asphalt lot. "You can take a tour up to the top with a guide on a bus. It's the only way they allow tourists up there. Looks like it's gotten real popular."

"Do we have to take a tour bus?" Kendall asked. This wasn't how he had pictured it.

"No, your great-grandfather gave me directions and told me to bring you directly to his home. We can go up the road on foot."

It seemed such a private place, Kendall wondered how they could stand to have people come and stare at their homes. A person could drive by on I-40 and not even know that miles across the countryside a people lived way up on top of a rock.

"They needed revenue," Dad explained. "Dry farming doesn't bring in a real good living. Tourism brings in a lot more money."

"Well, goodbye, kiddo. Be good," Brett said to Kendall. "I'm glad it's you and not me. Just being here makes me feel claustrophobic. There's too much space. Give me a city or town any day."

Kendall rolled his eyes at him. "Like, we live in a big city right now."

"At least there are stores and two-lane streets." Brett jumped out and went to find the rest rooms and a Coke machine.

Dad turned off the engine and twisted around to look at Kendall.

Kendall had already climbed over the bench seat to dig out his duffel bag. His father watched him, and he could feel the emotion strung out between them.

Dad sniffed and wiped his mouth. "Ready, buddy?"

Kendall slowly rose from the bed. "I guess." He wanted to say, "Don't cry, Dad," but he didn't. He took a big breath and held it in. It was harder than he had thought it would be. He was afraid that if he even said it, he'd start to cry himself.

Kendall finally hauled himself out of the truck and Dad locked the doors.

"Here," Dad said, hoisting the duffel bag onto his shoulder. "Let's take a walk. Actually, it's gonna be a hike."

Another white bus full of tourists drove slowly up the road in front of the visitor's center then circled around the south side of the mesa. After crossing the highway, Kendall followed his father up the half mile of road.

Golden boulders littered the landscape, some as big as the buildings in downtown Albuquerque. The rock formations were so huge it was hard not to stand and just stare. Giants who might whisper stories if only they could speak.

After the straight stretch, the road curved and began its ascent. From here, Kendall couldn't see the visitor's center. The bus was long gone and another wasn't due for half an hour. The only sound was their own footsteps on the gravelly concrete.

The last five hundred yards were the steepest, and they slowed way down, not even able to speak. Dad huffed and puffed with the duffel bag over his back. Kendall kept his head up, anticipation like a teeming ant bed in his gut, as the last part of the road turned to dirt and the pueblo loomed in front of his eyes. Long rows of ancient homes linked together had been built up to the edge of the cliff. Walking the dusty rock paths that wound through the brown, earthen homes, Kendall felt like he was entering a different world.

He had entered another dimension as well. Something aged and endless, eternity stretching backward and forward all at the same time.

Dad led him past the tour group. The guide, a girl about eighteen wearing jeans and a blouse, showed the people with hats and cameras how the adobe houses were constructed. A section of a wall had been left open to display the straw and mud bricks, plastered smooth with another layer of brown mud. He heard her say, ". . . all still done by hand . . ." before they turned again.

As they neared the end of the row, Dad stopped in the middle of the dirt street, shaking his head. "It feels strange to be here again. It's been a long time. I feel like I'm trespassing."

Kendall glanced at his father's face.

Dad had been chewing so hard on his lips, they were raw. "I'm not sure he would want to see me. I'm . . ." Dad stopped and swung the duffel bag off his shoulder. "I'm too different. I stick out here."

Kendall's head filled with mixed-up thoughts. His dad belonged with his own family, back in the Anglo world. His mother belonged here, in skin and language and knowledge and heart.

Kendall belonged nowhere. He was called Indian by his Drennan cousins, coyote or half-breed by the kids at school, but he didn't feel like either of those things. He didn't look completely Acoma, either. And he didn't know whether being half Anglo would cancel out his Acoma blood to his great-grandfather.

The street was bare. Silence hung about the adobe walls of the two-storied homes on both sides.

Dad pointed up ahead. "The letter said his home was on the second story of the last house on the right."

"Maybe I should go by myself," Kendall said.

Dad rubbed his mouth. "I hate to desert you, son. I just don't know if Armando Abeyta would want to see me."

"I can do it," Kendall said to reassure him. "Maybe it would be better."

His dad nodded slowly. "You sure?"

Kendall looked at his dad's face, noticing the spot where he'd missed with the razor. The reddish stubble sparkled under the sunlight.

Dad set the bag down onto the dirt. "I hate this, buddy," he said, and his voice cracked. "I'm going to miss you every day."

Kendall swallowed hard.

"Okay." Dad breathed out. "I'm okay. I'm not going to be a crybaby out here with all the neighbors to see. Mind your manners, clean your plate. You know—all that stuff." He stopped talking and grabbed Kendall into a big hug.

Kendall smashed his face into his father's plaid shirt. He smelled soap and cornflakes, and with a suddenness that surprised him, he smelled his mother's scent. He pulled back quickly. The smell was so sharp, the memory so intense, he knew it would unravel him quicker than anything else.

"Okay," Dad said again, "I'll get going so I can earn my paycheck. Hopefully no flat tires, huh?"

Kendall could only nod, fingering the straps of the duffel as he hefted the bag onto his shoulder.

"I'll write," Dad called back, jamming his hands into his jeans. "And you know my truck number in case of—you know—anything."

Grasping the wooden ladder, Kendall climbed the rungs to the first roof. From up here he could see the straight rows of homes and the square plaza two streets over. At the other end of the village, Kendall saw a huge old church with massive adobe walls. A bell tower complete with an actual bell adorned the top. How had people managed to carry the timber up the cliffs to build such a church?

He turned back to the home in front of him and reached out to touch the walls.

Before he could knock, Kendall heard someone singing a sort of chant behind the door. He didn't understand the words, but it made him feel as though his mother was whispering encouragement in his ear.

"It's Kendall," he called. "I am Rebecca's son."

Silence waited with the wind.

"*Ki-ya.* Am I welcome?" Kendall softly added, remembering the Acoma manners and expressions his mother had once taught him.

The door opened and an ancient-looking man stood there holding a walking stick, the face of a hissing rattlesnake carved into the wood. Deep-set brown eyes watched Kendall, the folded skin of his lids like a hood. Wearing jeans, a silver-buckled belt, and a blue shirt, his great-grandfather was shorter than his father but broader, with wide shoulders and a thick chest.

Armando Abeyta's face was wrinkled like a shriveled prickly pear cactus. Silver and turquoise adorned his neck and wrists, but most spectacular was his long white hair, parted in the middle and reaching clear to his waist. To keep his hair in place, he had knotted a red bandanna around his forehead.

"*Op-na.* Come in."

His great-grandfather's voice sounded like the rushing of a great river—old and immense.

The elderly man stepped aside to let Kendall cross the threshold, but as he did, Kendall quickly glanced backward. His eyes stung again.

Dad hadn't left. He still stood on the dusty street, watching. Kendall saw him pull his shoulders back and attempt an encouraging smile. Jaw clenched, cheek muscles twitching, his father raised a hand. Armando Abeyta lifted his hand in return and nodded. The two men watched each other for a moment; then Dad turned and walked back down the road.

Kendall blinked hard as the door closed behind him. At first he expected the adobe home would be completely dark, since it had only one window in the front, but the room wasn't as dim as he expected.

Blankets and jewelry hung from pegs on sparkling white-washed walls. A pot simmered on a woodstove. Next to the fire pit an adobe bench had been shaped right out of the wall. Colorful blankets spread across it like a couch.

"Put your bag in this corner," his great-grandfather told him in that deep voice. "There is only one bedroom, so this main room next to the kitchen will be yours. I have a sleeping bag and blankets for a mattress."

"Thanks," Kendall whispered, slipping his duffel bag off his arm.

Armando Abeyta stood in the center of the room, his long white hair brushing his belt. The hooded eyes watched Kendall, who wanted to squirm and run out the door after Dad.

"We have waited long to meet, you and I," Armando began.

Kendall nodded. He wanted to look around at the feathers and things hanging on the walls, but didn't dare to turn his head.

"There will be much to talk about over the next weeks," the old man added.

There were more moments of silence. Kendall heard the pot hiss on the woodstove.

Armando stepped closer. "Come, boy, let us walk."

Kendall followed him through the screen door and out onto the roof again. The sunlight was bright after the shadowy home. They climbed down the ladder back to the road.

The street was deserted. The entire village seemed empty. Were there people behind those adobe brick walls and smudged windows?

"Most of the year the village sleeps," his great-grandfather said.

"Are there people in all the houses?"

"A few spend the year living here as the ancients did. The others live in the villages of Acomita and McCartys in the valley ten miles to the north."

He stopped talking as he wound his way through the narrow, quiet streets, avoiding the tour groups. Kendall caught glimpses of tourists at the plaza and the church, groups of people with cameras stopping at tables where women sold pottery and jewelry.

"We have arrived," Armando said suddenly.

Kendall swallowed and glanced at him.

The door to one of the first-level homes swung open and a woman about his mother's age beckoned them inside. A girl stood at the kitchen table boxing pottery bowls and figures. She looked at Kendall through thick black bangs and picked up her box.

"Mary," Armando said firmly. "Here is the boy. This is what you wanted and you have it. Now I have things to do."

Kendall watched his great-grandfather cross the brick floor and leave, banging the screen door and disappearing into the glaring sunshine.

Before Kendall could follow, the woman quickly came forward. "Hello, little cousin," she said in a soft voice. Her straight dark hair, clipped back with a wide clasp at her neck, fell nearly to her knees, reminding him of his mother's hair. "I'm Mary Ramirez, your mother's second cousin. We were the same age and Rebecca didn't have any other cousins. I've been wanting to meet you for a long time."

Kendall felt as if the polite words he should say were stuck in his throat. He was still trying to take in his great-grandfather's abrupt departure. His great-grandfather was the one who had sent for him, after all.

Mrs. Ramirez sensed his unease. "It is hard for him," she said. "Just give him time." She gestured to the girl. "This is my daughter, Trina."

Kendall looked around, noticing the woodstove, no lights, no refrigerator, no television. "Do you live here all the time? He—Armando—said only a few people do. Where is everybody else?"

"A few people come to Old Acoma to sell our pottery,

but we live in Acomita and Trina goes to school there. There's electricity and running water. Homes just like you're used to." She smiled at Kendall. "On feast days, Sky City becomes alive with all the families and clans and there are dances. It can be a hard life living four hundred feet in the air," Mary added in her quiet voice. "Your great-grandfather is not like most."

Kendall felt a moment of panic. Was it too late to catch Dad? What was he doing here? What had he been thinking? He wondered if Mary would let him stay with them in Acomita even though they had just met. He knew now that his great-grandfather didn't really want him here.

"I don't get it," he finally choked out. "Why did he write that letter asking me to come?"

Mary looked away, brushing a hand against her hair nervously. "I'm the one that convinced him. Twenty years is too long not to forgive. It has been especially difficult for Armando since his wife died two months ago. He promised her he would contact you. But your great-grandfather had me write the letter to your father and I signed his name."

A lead weight sank to the bottom of Kendall's stomach. The letter that Dad assumed Armando had written had actually been forged. Did Dad know that? He couldn't have, or he never would have brought Kendall.

"Many years ago I met your older brother. He was just a baby. Rebecca brought him, but she didn't stay more than a few hours. It was not good." Mary shook her head and waved away the words. "Your brother looked just like your father. But you, Kendall. I can't believe how much you look like Rebecca." She stopped and bit her lip. "I'm so glad you're here."

Kendall felt a little sick. She was the only one who was glad. How was he going to survive the next six weeks without Dad? Forty-two days. It might as well be forty-two years.

Mary turned to Trina. "I'm taking these pieces to Corinne at the plaza. Why don't you take Kendall on a tour of Sky City?"

The girl dug her hands into the pockets of her jeans and nodded. She hadn't said two words since their introduction.

Kendall wasn't sure how she felt about it, but it turned out that once the grown-ups were gone, she wasn't as shy as she first appeared. In fact, just the opposite.

5

"**H**ang on to my arm and look over the cliff," Trina ordered. "Don't worry, you won't fall."

Kendall raised an eyebrow. "Right. Like you're strong enough to hang on to me."

"I'm incredibly strong," Trina told him evenly. She was his height, skinny with legs like sticks in her jeans. After she had given him the unofficial tour, they ended up at the edge of the mesa.

Kendall's head spun when he leaned over and saw clear to the desert floor below. His sneakers skidded, throwing pebbles over the edge. They bounced on the rocks, then echoed off the canyon walls.

Just then Trina's fingers slipped and Kendall lost his balance. He cried out and grabbed her arm to keep from falling, then landed on his rear end.

She laughed at him.

Kendall scrambled to his feet. "It's not funny." Her long straight bangs swung across the top of his eyes—eyes that reminded him of his mother.

"Sorry, I was just trying to get a better grip when my

36

hand slipped," Trina apologized. "You weren't really going to fall, but heights make me feel dizzy, too." She got on her knees, hung her upper body over the edge, and pointed downward. "If you look close, you can see the spots of blood when Zaldivar and his soldiers stormed Acoma."

Taking no chances, Kendall got on his stomach and wriggled up to Trina's side. Red spots sprinkled the rocks below. It really did look like splattered blood. "Is that Zaldivar's blood, and his men's?"

"No." Trina lowered her voice. "Acoma blood."

"What do you mean?" Kendall asked. "When did this happen?"

"Hundreds of years ago. Back when the Spanish conquerors came in 1598. They were always demanding food and supplies until the pueblos ran out of food themselves. One day Zaldivar's brother and a few soldiers arrived. The warriors ended up killing the soldiers. Zaldivar got revenge bigtime. There was a battle, and he ruined the fields and burned everyone's homes."

Kendall stared at her. "That's awful."

Trina gave him a chilling smile. "It gets worse. All the warriors were locked up in the kivas. Then Zaldivar took them one by one from the kivas, murdered them, and threw them over the cliffs."

"You're kidding—that's pretty gruesome." Kendall wasn't sure whether to believe her or not.

"All the girls had to go work for the Spaniards for twenty-five years. The older men that hadn't been thrown over the cliffs had to be their servants for twenty-five years, too, plus the Spaniards cut one of the feet off each of them as punishment."

"Cut off their feet?"

"The blood still stains the rocks," Trina told him. "Not

even the rain gods wash it away when they send their storms."

The wind ruffled the hair on the back of Kendall's neck. Her words raised goose bumps, making him shiver.

"I would rather have had both my feet chopped off than become a servant in Zaldivar's army." In a spooky voice she added, "Picture the trail of bloody stumps descending the paths of Acoma, never to return."

"You're making it up," Kendall finally said.

"It's all true," Trina assured him. "Ask anyone. Ask the cacique."

"Who's that?"

"The pueblo chief. That's probably where Great-uncle is right now. He spends a lot of time talking to the elders. He's the oldest man at Acoma."

"Okay, okay, I believe you," Kendall said. No way was he going to talk to the chief.

"But cutting off their feet is not all the Spanish conquerors did."

"You mean there's more?"

"They took away our names."

"Nobody can do that."

"The priests baptized everybody and then gave them new, Spanish names. Nobody was allowed to speak their native language. But," Trina said, pausing, her eyes shining, "everybody kept secret names and spoke Keresan in secret when the Spaniards weren't around."

Kendall felt a little lightbulb go on in his head. His mother had given him an Acoma name, something private just between the two of them. He hadn't heard his Indian name in so long he could barely even remember how to pronounce it. Mom hadn't used it very often. But the tradition was still alive, hundreds of years later. There was something secure and comforting in knowing that.

"Acoma was almost wiped out for a while," Trina said. "All the fighting, plus diseases and stuff."

Flat on their stomachs, heads over the edge of the crevice, they talked to each other as if they were in a backyard having a casual chat, and yet they were four hundred feet in the air. It was a strange feeling.

"Do you try to scare everyone that comes to visit?" he asked. "You should be an actress or something."

"I'm just practicing for when I can be a tour guide. They tell this story on the tour, but nobody can tell it like I can."

"I believe it."

"They call this Dead Man's Trail," Trina said, pointing. "See, there's the path."

Kendall wouldn't have called the worn places on the rocks a path. "Was it named Dead Man's Trail because people die trying to get up and down the cliffs?"

"No, there was a warrior who hid at the top of the trail. He sounded the alarm when he spotted the army. Then he shot arrows at the soldiers, but there were too many of them. They had guns and cannons. The warrior was killed. Sometimes they call this path Runner's Trail. It was used by runners sent out to spy on the Spanish armies."

Kendall sat up. *Runner's Trail.*

"But don't you think Dead Man's Trail sounds scarier?"

Getting to his feet, Kendall stared out over the cliff to Enchanted Mesa three miles away. The two mesas were like sisters, one straight and tall with no paths or access to the summit, while Sky City was rounder, with her small hidden paths and foot and handholds to reach the smooth table top.

He longed to run to Enchanted Mesa and could feel the powerful stirring of the magic. It hadn't stopped since he'd arrived. He also wanted to see the horse again, but Trina's mother, Mary Ramirez, appeared beside them with a bucket and a spade.

"It's time to go digging," she told her daughter, then turned to Kendall. "Can you use a shovel?"

"Sure. What are we going to do?" Kendall asked.

"Come and I'll show you," Mary said.

Kendall watched Trina's mother, his own mother's second cousin, as they took the path down the back of the mesa. The woman was silent, her hair knotted into a pile on her head for working just the way Mom used to wear hers. She was also about the same height as his mother, but a little plumper, especially as his mother had grown so thin during her last few months.

"Mom doesn't talk when she's dreaming up the design for her next pot," Trina told Kendall. "We need to find more clay to make the pottery that we sell to the tourists during the summertime."

"Who's selling right now when you're digging?"

"My older sister, Corinne," Trina explained. "She's trying to sell a lot this summer to save for college next year. But I like digging for the clay."

After climbing down the back trail, Mary stopped at a hollow at the base of Sky City. "This would be a good day for firing if we had our pots made," she said. "No wind, no clouds, but today we need to concentrate on finding the clay that is waiting inside the earth."

"Come on," Trina said to Kendall. "Let's look over there under those rocks." She brushed aside stones and dirt. Kendall turned over the earth with the shovel wherever she pointed out a spot, but their first few tries revealed only sand.

A few minutes later Mary beckoned them to the boulders at the base of the mesa. Kendall stuck in the shovel again, pushing it down with his foot. The crust was harder here, but when he lifted out the soil and turned it over, Trina said, "Oh, that's it!"

A milky-white layer stained the reddish-brown earth.

"Mom, I think this is good."

Mary knelt down to inspect it with her fingers, then nodded her approval. "It is good." She stood again and Kendall began to dig deeper into the spot. Mary reached over and put a hand on the shovel to stop him. "We must pray before we begin," she explained. "Each time we come to dig, Mother Earth gives of her flesh. If we don't pray, the clay will disappear."

There was a pause and Kendall wondered if he should close his eyes like in church, but Trina and her mother didn't. Instead, Mary was silent for a few moments as if listening to the land around them.

Kendall heard the breeze touch the rocks. Insects buzzed in crevices under the brush. The sun was hot on his back.

He watched, intrigued, as Mary held out a fist in front of her body, then opened her hand, sprinkling a fine yellow dust onto the ground.

Kendall was surprised, unaware that she had been carrying something with her.

Trina whispered, "It's sacred cornmeal."

Mary's voice was tender when she spoke at last. "Thank you, Mother Earth, for giving your clay to us. Help us discover the life and shapes within it, and may you give us more from your belly for our future days."

Kendall watched Trina gazing at her mother as the woman expressed her thanks and hopes. He could tell they had done this many times together and he tried to bite back the feeling rising in his chest. Mostly it was a sharp longing. He knew he would never be able to share Acoma with his mother and pray over the earth. Trina had a place here, no other blood to make her different. She knew she belonged with the people of the pueblo, within her clan and family, and she always would.

All he knew how to do was run, but the only Acomas that had ever run were spies hundreds of years ago. He didn't know anything about the things he'd seen here, their pottery or ceremonial dress. Even the way they baked bread in the outdoor ovens was foreign to him.

He had a desire that didn't fit. He didn't know where it came from, but he did know he wanted to belong here, and he wanted this place to become familiar.

"Dig up the rocks and then I'll scoop out the clay into this bucket," Mary instructed.

Kendall stuck the shovel in and removed a big pile of rocks and dirt. Underneath, the soil turned a whitish gray.

"That's the clay," Trina said.

"It's like brick, it's so hard."

Trina knelt and scooped out the dry, lumpy stuff into her five-gallon bucket. "We soak the clay in water, then knead it until it gets soft. After that we can start making our bowls and animals."

"It must take a long time."

"Working with clay is slow," Mary agreed, coming up behind them to inspect their digging. "But time and patience make it a gift back to the earth."

Trina tapped her spade against the bucket. "I'll show you my mom's story bowls. Lots of people buy them. I love making the little animals, especially turtles and lizards."

After filling the second bucket, Kendall dragged it over to Mary for approval. He almost knocked the entire thing onto the ground when he saw the white horse suddenly appear in the distance, galloping and prancing like a dancer.

"There she is," he said, letting out a breath. "Look."

Trina raised her head. "That's Rasmiyah, my horse."

"*Your* horse?" Kendall said, feeling his heart sink.

"Of course she's mine," Trina shot back. "I've seen her the last few months, running wild. I've named her, and she belongs to me."

"Have you ever ridden her?"

"No, she's wild. You can't ride a wild horse."

Trina's superior attitude bugged Kendall. Of course he knew the horse was wild. She wore no bit or halter, and she had the freedom of the earth and the sky in her eyes. He took one small step forward and Rasmiyah turned and bolted for the horizon.

"But you could tame a wild horse. Just a little to touch them," Kendall said.

"I claimed her, and I can decide to tame her or not," Trina replied. "Besides, I've already tried to catch her, and she's not tameable. So don't even bother to try."

"I could race her," Kendall said quietly. "I could run like a horse and race with her across the desert."

"No one can race against a horse. They run faster than people, and they can run longer. Probably a hundred miles before they get tired."

Kendall couldn't help disagreeing, even though he really didn't know. "A wild horse doesn't run for miles and miles, just in bursts to get away from the people trying to catch them."

He felt Trina eyeing him. "I bet you couldn't even race against me," she challenged.

Kendall glanced over, startled. "Sure I could."

"I run the hundred-yard dash faster than anyone else at Acomita Elementary."

"No way," Kendall said, not believing her.

"Race you right now. To that boulder out there by the scrub oak."

Trina took off before Kendall could even reply. He dropped the shovel at Mary's feet and sprinted after Trina.

She had a good head start and wasn't slowing down a bit. Kendall poured on the speed. The stone was farther away than it looked. It felt like several hundred-yard dashes all strung together, and still Trina was ahead of him.

The boulder grew bigger the closer he got, and as they neared it, Kendall reached out just as Trina did. They both slapped the rough surface, tagging it at the very same moment.

Panting, Trina folded her arms across her chest. "Surprised you, didn't I?"

He gasped, "You're lucky to run longer distances at your school."

"I want to run track at Grant's High School some day," Trina said, shaking out her legs. "They have good teams there and in Gallup."

Leaning against the boulder, Kendall sighed as he watched the white horse gallop across the desert for Enchanted Mesa, tail straight out in the wind. The rock mesa looked like a beautiful white island rising on a sea of grass.

Kendall couldn't stop from speaking his thoughts out loud. "I want to run to Enchanted Mesa and catch Rasmiyah." It was the wrong thing to say.

Trina lifted her chin. "You can't catch her," she told him. "Even if you had the chance, I bet you couldn't get close to her."

Kendall didn't reply for a moment, feeling the magical lure the wind carried. "I bet I could," he said finally, trying not to let Trina get to him. "I know I will."

6

For dinner, Mary Ramirez brought Kendall and Armando stew and bread freshly baked in the adobe ovens before she and her daughters left Sky City and returned to their house at Acomita.

"How soon will you be back?" Kendall asked, trying to keep his aunt there longer.

"You'll see us tomorrow," Mary said reassuringly. "If you get tired of sponge baths or want to use the telephone, just let me know."

Armando muttered something at her last words, and Mary said, "Oh, Uncle. You should come down off Sky City sometime and have a bath in a real tub and watch the news on television."

The elderly man ignored her comments.

"You'll come visit us sometime," Mary told Kendall.

Trina was silent. After their conversation about Rasmi-yah, Kendall wondered if she had decided not to speak to him.

The sun was beginning to set, but Armando hadn't lit any of the kerosene lamps. A small fire on the open hearth gave off a yellow glow, enough light to throw shadows against the white walls but little heat.

Kendall helped his great-grandfather clean up the kitchen, using water from a barrel kept in the corner. Acoma was both not what he expected and exactly what he had expected all at the same time. A place where people kept to themselves and yet knew each other well.

"I've been watching Enchanted Mesa," Kendall said as he finished drying the cups. The silence was getting to him and he had to say something or he'd bust. "Trina said the pueblo used to live on top of it. But how did people get up and down?"

"I'm surprised Trina didn't tell you the story. She likes danger and blood."

Kendall watched him from the corner of his eye. There was a hint of a smile on his great-grandfather's face, but it quickly left again.

Armando Abeyta laid the dish rag out to dry, then went into the main room and sat cross-legged against the hard wall. "It looks like it's just you and me, boy."

Kendall stood awkwardly next to his duffel bag and bedroll. He didn't know what he was expected to do.

The fire spit a flurry of sparks and Armando began to speak. "Long before Sky City existed, when our people first emerged from the underworld, they built a village on Katzima, the Enchanted Mesa."

Kendall felt tingles run down his back as he pictured a pueblo village on top of that tall white rock.

"Get blankets to sit on," his great-grandfather added, interrupting himself. "It is time for our evening stories, and this is important, so listen well."

Kendall retrieved three of the colorful wool blankets from a stack in the corner, giving two to the old man and spreading one out for himself.

"The people called themselves Ako and descended the mesa to tend their fields during the day, returning to their homes on Katzima at night."

"But how did they climb to the top?" Kendall asked. "I didn't see any paths."

Armando raised a hand, signaling Kendall to be patient. "One spring while most of the village was planting the fields, a terrible storm came, the worst storm ever seen with thunder, lightning, and rain. The ground quivered and a mighty wind destroyed the Ladder Trail. Tons of rock thundered down the side of the mesa. The village was ruined. Swept off. With the path gone, there was no way to save the few women stranded on top."

The fire crackled, and Kendall pictured the entire village carried off in a tornado.

"The Great Spirits did not want us to live on Katzima any longer, so they put their enchantments upon it. Any remaining path twists and turns, entangling all who try to climb. Once you get to the top, you can never find your way back. But the gods blessed us when they provided Sky City."

"We have been in this valley on top of our mesas before the Spaniard's Christ ever lived in Jerusalem. *Ako* means 'a place that always was.' This is our eternal home."

In the firelight, Kendall studied his great-grandfather's face. Two deep lines ran down the middle of each cheek like the ridges on the walls of Acoma. The past of this man spanned almost a century. He'd seen the beginnings of cars, airplanes, television, and computers. Yet he lived without plumbing or electricity. Kendall had to get used to the village outhouses on the edge of the cliffs real quick.

Then Kendall worked up the courage to ask the question he really wanted to know. "What was my mother like growing up here?"

Armando paused so long, Kendall thought he wasn't going to answer. But when he did, he wouldn't even look at his great-grandson.

"I do not like to speak of those who live in the spirit world." He broke off suddenly. "Help me. I prefer the floor, but I cannot get there or back very easily."

Trying not to let Armando's rebuff bother him, Kendall jumped up and held out his arms, but the old man did not rise at once. He gripped Kendall's hands and studied his palms, then turned them over. "You have a lot of your father. Perhaps some of my granddaughter, your mother, is there also. But only time will tell me if this is true."

Kendall leaned back to pull the elderly man to his feet. He could feel the dry skin of the old man's twisted fingers in his own.

"People say a man of ninety-five lives a long and happy life. When you get this old, it just means you have seen your family go on without you. Being the last one may not be so fortunate."

Kendall had no answer as his great-grandfather walked into the back room. After Armando closed the bedroom door, Kendall slowly unrolled the sleeping bag. He stripped off his clothes and lay on his stomach, burying his head in his pillow.

His great-grandfather's last words bothered him. His hidden message seemed to be full of questions and challenges. How could Kendall prove himself? What was expected of him?

He got up to close the front door. Cool air drifted through the screen. Under the starlight, he saw shadows of the homemade ladders reaching to the rooftops.

He'd never been in such a quiet place before. No distant radio music or hum of traffic and sirens. Not even any voices.

Armando Abeyta had said everyone he loved had already gone ahead of him to the spirit world. But what about him, his great-grandson?

A wave of homesickness hit Kendall like a stomachache. He thought about Dad and Brett on their way across Arizona. What were they doing tonight? Sleeping in the truck or a motel? For a moment he even missed Brett. How could he last forty-two more days?

Kendall closed the door, embarrassed to be in just his underclothes. He touched the sashes and blankets hanging as decorations on the walls. Bundles of smooth sticks, notched where soft feathers had been tied, were called prayer sticks, Armando had told him.

In one dark corner a few pictures of feast days had been hung in groups on the wall. In the photos, dancers moved to the drumbeat in colorful ceremonial dress. Bracelets, rings, and necklaces adorned their necks and hands.

The last photo was an old black-and-white of a splendid young man, a dark blanket wrapped high about his shoulders. A bandanna made from the same material had been folded and knotted around his head. Straight black hair lay flat against his cheeks, two inches below his ears.

There were those eyes. The same eyes as his great-grandfather, piercing right through the old photo in its tin frame. Kendall stepped back, as if the man were actually looking at him, reading his mind. This had to be Armando as a young man. But when? Kendall counted backward in his head. Sometime in the 1920s.

But the man inside the photo could have been an Acoma man from a hundred years ago.

Or perhaps even a thousand.

In the shadows next to the picture, farther away from the fire, hung a deerskin bag, drawstrings closed tight. Without taking it off its hook, Kendall turned the bag in his hands, feeling the soft old buckskin. The bag was empty and he wondered what it had been used for.

When he laid the pouch back against the wall, Kendall heard a clunk. Fearing he'd broken something, Kendall gently lifted it up to look. No damage had been done. The bag had only been placed in front of a framed print that shifted when he moved the pouch, hitting the hard wall. Its position made him wonder if the picture had deliberately been hidden. Kendall tried to make out what it was, but the light was too shadowy. Carefully he took the wooden frame down from its nail.

One look at the picture and Kendall sucked in his breath. His heart pounded as he pulled the old photo closer to the fire's dim light.

Four men dressed only in loincloths stood barefoot on the dusty earth. A barren rock ridge hovered in the background. Kendall stared at each man, at their solemn, unsmiling faces, black hair straight to the shoulders and heads wrapped and tied with bandannas.

Each man's sinewy arms, legs, and chest had been streaked with white paint. Lightning bolts ran down their thighs.

Acoma Runners. These words had been handwritten at the bottom, and a date, 19 something, smudged by a water stain.

Kendall studied each man, then moved back to the portrait of his great-grandfather to compare. The man in the middle of the group of barefoot runners was Armando Abeyta, thigh muscles taut and lean.

His great-grandfather was an Acoma runner.

The magic strings tightened their grip.

7

There was no clock in the house, so Kendall didn't know what time it was when he woke up. The magic had been building and building ever since he had jumped out of the truck three days ago and run to Enchanted Mesa.

Three days of awkward silences and stiff conversations, along with three nights of trying not to cry in his pillow. It took forever to go to sleep and Kendall felt like a baby.

He had spent the days lounging around or checking out the jewelry and pottery tables. Soon he knew the prices and the names of the women who sold. They didn't say much, just watched him with quiet, dark eyes.

A couple of times he fell into step with a tour group and took the official Sky City tour. When it was time to take the bus down the hill, he slunk off and went down the cliff trail, finding a cubbyhole in the rock in which to sit and keep cool. Kendall daydreamed about Dad and Brett and what they might be doing each day. Every day the loneliness grew worse.

He'd put off running, not knowing if he should. But this morning his legs wanted to fly out of the pueblo and run and run. He couldn't resist the demanding lure of the magic any longer.

Kendall didn't care anymore what Armando or Trina or anyone else thought. He got up and peeked again at the photo hidden under the pouch. What did the lightning symbols mean? He wanted to learn everything, but Kendall didn't know if it was proper to ask. If only he could go back in time and be a runner with them. He finally stepped back from the photo, heart thudding. This was his time to run, though.

Kendall yanked a T-shirt over his head. Shorts, socks, and Nikes went on in seconds. Then he got himself a drink of water and ate a hunk of leftover bread.

Cool morning air rushed in when he swung open the door. Sunrise glinted off the east mountains and Kendall watched shadows from the night creep over the valley.

He picked his way down the trail on the west side that he had taken with Trina, past the thousand-ton boulders. After warming up, Kendall turned east toward Katzima.

He was used to sprinting, racing across finish lines, hurrying home. He had to keep reining himself in, slowing to a jog, or he'd never make it all the way to Enchanted Mesa.

It wasn't long until he had a pain in his side. He kept going, trying to breathe evenly, but the pain doubled him over. Kendall gasped and clutched his thighs to keep from falling.

He raised his head to see how close he was just as the sun roared over the distant mountains. The golden light bathed Enchanted Mesa—so brilliant, Kendall had to squint from the glare.

He glanced back at Sky City. One lazy spiral of smoke curled into the air. Someone getting an early start on bread-making before the tours began. Fresh round loaves of bread would be sold later for a couple of bucks.

When Kendall faced east again, Enchanted Mesa seemed as far away as ever. Hadn't he run farther than that?

Kendall had to walk a long ways before the stitch in his side eased and he could jog once more.

The terrain that looked so flat from Sky City was actually rocky in places. Soft sand occasionally pulled at his sneakers. Kendall picked up the pace, dodging wild brush and tumbleweeds. He had to be careful to miss the gopher holes that pockmarked the ground and the cholla cactus that snagged him if he brushed too close.

Sweat poured down his face as Kendall watched the mesa grow closer. In the dawn, the white walls appeared yellow, streaked by red.

His legs felt like bricks. The cramp was back again. Kendall pushed on, trying to keep his stride even so that the pain didn't completely stop him.

The mesa grew bigger the closer he got, and Kendall had to raise his eyes to see the top. It was completely flat, as if someone, perhaps God himself, had sanded it. The thought surprised him. It must be the immense quiet. When he ran, he could hear his shoes hitting the earth and his hoarse breath, but when he stopped, the silence was overwhelming.

He was nearly there. The terrain grew rockier. More and more scrub and piñon trees stood in his way. In places it was like dodging through a forest of juniper bushes.

At last he reached the rocky perimeter and stopped running. But once he stopped, he found it hard to stand. His legs shook like a wind-up toy and he had to sit down or he'd fall right into the cactus.

Taking three more steps, Kendall dropped onto the dirt, closing his eyes. His heart slammed against his ribs. There in the shade of a scrub oak, Kendall could have passed out, he was so tired, but he also felt elated.

He'd done it. Hung on to the cord and run three miles across the desert.

After several minutes Kendall felt ants crawling across his arms and sat up. His head didn't spin quite so fast and he could stand, although his throat hurt now. It was stupid not to think of bringing water. This wasn't like running at home with a hose at the end of the journey. He kicked at the piles of rocks and found a smooth, gray stone. After wiping the rock clean on his shorts, Kendall stuck it in his mouth to suck on.

Hands on his hips, Kendall studied the mounds of rubble piled around the base. The debris was like a shield, barring a person from touching the mesa itself. But Kendall was determined to put his hands on the rock.

He slipped through the soft sand filled with rock and boulders. The gravel defied him to keep going. His feet slid backward and Kendall caught himself, slicing his palm. Speckles of blood dried up quickly in the heat and Kendall rubbed his hand against his shorts.

Perhaps there was an easier spot. He backed off and surveyed the mesa. Farther south the talus wasn't quite as deep, so Kendall headed there.

He scrambled upward, filling his shoes with sand, then finally grabbed the rock side of the mesa and hung on, trying to keep his balance on the small spot. He didn't want to slide right down into the boulders. Then he'd really be a bloody mess.

As he looked up at the straight walls, the sun slanted sideways and blue sky winked through the cracks. Kendall felt like a bug next to a mountain. He wondered where the original trail had been that the storm destroyed hundreds of years ago. The walls were so vertical, he couldn't see how anybody had possibly climbed them.

Kendall picked his way down until he was on flat ground

again. He chose a pale purple boulder and sat down, using the rock for a headrest. Scanning the wild brush of Acoma Valley, Kendall could see for miles.

A ring of ridged mesas enclosed the entire valley like a cocoon. Twenty-five miles to the north, mist covered the peaks of Mount Taylor.

His legs had stopped trembling, but his head jerked as he tried to stay awake. Sun heated his arms and the scent of juniper filled his nose. Insects buzzed in the distance. He watched a butterfly weave around a patch of prickly pear cactus.

The valley was hushed; it seemed to belong just to him. The early morning smoke curls were gone now. From a distance, the adobe apartment houses disappeared completely, as if the city had vanished.

His muscles cramped when he got up, and Kendall knew he was going to be sore tomorrow. Shaking out his legs, he began to walk around the mesa, picking his way through the rubble of boulders and stones. Shadows and sunlight played on every angle of Enchanted Mesa.

As Kendall came around to the south again, he squinted into the bright sunlight. Something was coming toward him across the valley. Was it Rasmiyah? His heart surged with hope and he shaded his eyes.

A lone figure, walking with a staff, headed straight for him. Armando Abeyta's long white hair swung in a braid down his back. The old man walked methodically, back straight, barely using the carved wooden cane for support.

Conscious of his dirty knees and sweaty face, Kendall waited. Soon his great-grandfather's face came into clear view. The elderly man never hesitated, even missing the rocks and lumps hidden in the brush.

Sweat beaded the edges of the old man's bandanna and dark circles lined the underarms of his shirt. He picked a place to stop and dug the cane into the dirt to hold it upright. "You're up early, boy."

Kendall nodded, wondering if he'd done something wrong.

The black hooded eyes studied him. "Did you run or walk across the valley?"

"Ran mostly."

"You have the gut pains, don't you? Most people can't run more than a mile in the beginning."

Armando untied a red bandanna cloth wrapped around his arm. He folded it over until it made a narrow strip, then tied the cloth around Kendall's forehead, knotting it on the left side.

Kendall could feel the man's warm breath on his face as he worked. "Thank you," he said as his great-grandfather stepped back to survey him.

"You are foolish not to bring water into the desert."

"I forgot to pack a water bottle," Kendall admitted, feeling stupid. "But I cleaned a stone," he added, showing him. "I've been sucking on it."

Armando seemed to approve of the rock. He pulled the staff out of the earth and began walking north. Kendall followed him as they picked their way around the base of Enchanted Mesa, avoiding the slippery rocks. After half a mile the elderly man stopped to gaze at the deep crevices as though looking into the heart of the rock.

"Here," he said, reaching into the back of his belt. He pulled out a smoothly whittled stick, notched and tied with black-and-white feathers. "Take this prayer stick and wedge it into that upper crevice of Katzima. There are two footholds that will lift you several feet from the ground. Reach with your right hand into a crevice just above your head. Put this inside and return."

Armando placed the prayer stick into his hands. The

wood was soft as satin and beautifully crafted, and Kendall couldn't resist smoothing his fingers over the feathers. "You want me to take it up there?" Kendall asked, pointing to the straight, sheer walls. He swallowed. He wasn't a rock climber, and there was no one to give him a boost.

"It will be safer for you to climb than for me," his great-grandfather said, eyeing him. "Unless you don't think you're up to it."

Kendall glanced at the stick clutched in his hand. Without a word, he ventured across the mounds of rock up to the mesa walls again. He didn't care how clumsy he looked, he just didn't want to slip again, especially in front of Armando.

He put the prayer stick in the waistband of his shorts, then stuck his toes into the indentations and moved up the steep rock walls. Gulping in air, he hoisted himself and found another set of holes to go higher still, then glanced back.

His great-grandfather stood in the same spot, watching Kendall closely. He didn't call out directions or advice.

Kendall's nose scraped the rock as he pulled himself up. He felt his arms quivering and hoped he wouldn't fall backward. Clinging to the mesa, he let go with his right hand to feel for the hollow spot. Kendall patted the dust above his head and found the crevice. He reached down, pulled the feathered stick from his waist, and slid it into the hole.

There, it was done. Kendall stretched up as far as he dared and spotted the feathers safe inside the dim recesses of the rock. Grabbing the handhold near his chest again, Kendall tried to stop trembling so he could return to the ground.

He slowly inched his way down. Misjudging the distance the last two feet, Kendall stumbled to the bed of rocks, falling to his knees and ruining an almost perfect descent. He swiped at the blood, smearing it across his calf, and felt like a klutz.

But pride in accomplishing the task overcame the pain. Kendall felt as if he'd passed a test.

His great-grandfather didn't speak at first, just gazed at the mesa as if in silent prayer. "You did well," he finally grunted. "Let us sit here," he added and moved to a flat boulder facing the valley and Sky City.

Kendall sat next to him, smearing a finger over his knee to stop the bleeding. "Why do you put a prayer stick inside Enchanted Mesa?"

"Prayers are always left at sacred places," Armando said slowly. "The gods receive them there. Enchanted Mesa is a holy place to us. Next month the kachinas will be coming to Old Acoma. Physical and spiritual preparation is very important. Our hearts and bodies must be cleansed. I pray today to begin my personal preparation for what will happen this summer."

Kendall glanced over. "The kachinas are the gods, aren't they? I mean, people become like the gods behind the kachina masks. Something like that."

The elderly man searched his face. "How do you know this?"

"My mother told me. She showed me her kachina dolls all wrapped in special cloths. She said they come to the village during the summer with the rain dances."

A muscle in Armando Abeyta's face twitched as he set his mouth in a thin line. "Acoma is closed to the public during that time. No whites are allowed to see the gods."

8

Kendall froze. The words hung in the air, growing bigger with each imagined echo. Even his bloody knee seemed to inflate like a balloon.

His great-grandfather's knotty hands grew wider and tougher as they wrapped around the walking stick, which now looked thick as a tree trunk. All seemed to spell out how much Kendall didn't belong. Even the long white braid shooting down the old man's back was so different.

Kendall swallowed past his dry throat. The old man might be planning to send him away before July when they kicked the white people off Sky City. Kendall cringed at his own thoughts. They seemed so harsh. But he had dreamed of Acoma and his mother's stories for so long that he felt as if he already belonged. He wanted to belong. He wanted to be an Acoma runner. But even though he was here at last, he was still a stranger, an outsider.

His hopes of finding his mother were fast disappearing. Nothing spoke of her presence. Nothing seemed familiar. Nothing except the magic, and after today's run, that was beginning to feel like torture.

Kendall wanted to ask Armando about the running, but he didn't dare. There had to be a reason the picture was hidden. And the answers to why Kendall felt the urge to run were locked inside that picture.

"I'm going back," he said, rising to his feet. The silence between them was starting to swallow him up.

The old man didn't say anything, only pulled his staff closer to his leg.

As Kendall began to run again, he felt his great-grandfather's eyes on his back. Kendall tried to run straighter, taller, prouder, but after half a mile his shoulders slumped. He had to concentrate on putting one foot in front of the other. The three miles back felt like ten.

When he climbed the ladder to the Abeyta home, Kendall thought he was going to die. He couldn't even feel his legs anymore. He collapsed onto his sleeping bag, but he was desperate for water. Getting back to his feet, he staggered into the kitchen and dipped a cup into the drinking barrel. It was hard to swallow, his throat hurt so badly.

Back on the bedroll, he managed to peel off his sticky shirt before his head smacked the pillow. When he opened his eyes again, Kendall could hear singing nearby. The voice was soft and deep. Armando's voice. As his great-grandfather continued the soothing rhythm and words, Kendall dropped back into a dreamless sleep.

It was pitch-black when he woke up the second time. He tried to roll over and found his legs wouldn't move. Every muscle ached. How could he have been so stupid to run six miles all at once?

"Hey, hey," said a low voice from the darkness. Something cool brushed his face, and Kendall realized it was his great-grandfather's hands. Armando pressed a cup to his lips and Kendall drank some kind of herb tea. It scalded his throat. He felt ashamed to be such a wimp. One little run and he was out. Those Acoma runners looked so tough they could probably run a marathon without even breathing hard.

"What time is it?" he asked.

"Between night and dawn" was the reply.

"I slept for more than eighteen hours?" Kendall asked, his voice cracking.

Armando refilled the mug and watched as Kendall drank the whole thing. When he finished, Kendall began to feel better. He tested out his arms, swinging them above his head. So far, so good. His legs were a different story. But already he wanted to go back to Enchanted Mesa. He could feel the enchantments working on him again. The wild horse, Rasmiyah, was out there in the valley somewhere, and he wanted to see her, too.

His great-grandfather sat cross-legged on the adobe seat and placed his hands on his knees. "This is not the first time you have run. Nobody could make it across the valley on their first try."

"I have been running for a while," Kendall admitted.

"Why do you run, boy?"

Kendall paused. No one had asked him so bluntly before. He'd never explained the magic to anyone, only that one time with his mother, but she didn't know what he was talking about. It was a secret he kept to himself, but whenever he thought about the picture—those Acoma runners—he felt dizzy with the magic.

"Tell me why you run," his great-grandfather repeated.

Dawn crept into the room like fingers of pale yellow light.

Kendall thought about the power of the magic and knew he couldn't explain it. "It sounds silly."

Armando frowned. "Do you win trophies and medals with your running?"

Kendall shook his head. "No. I've never won a medal or anything." He stopped, feeling hurt that his great-grandfather would think he ran only to win first-place ribbons or to beat other opponents. "It's more important than that," he added.

But he wasn't sure if Armando heard him, and the distance between them was still awkward.

"Come, let us eat," his great-grandfather said abruptly. "It is time to walk to Katzima."

Kendall looked up. "I don't think I can walk."

Armando Abeyta rose and stood in front of him. "An Acoma runner can always run to Enchanted Mesa. Until the day he dies."

Acoma runners. Kendall wanted to ask about them, but it was hard when his great-grandfather looked like a warrior chief, even though he wore jeans and boots.

Kendall offered to scramble eggs in a pan over the wood-stove while Armando heated a pot of beans. They ate at the table in silence, finishing a round loaf of bread just as the sun rose over the ring of mountains.

Leaving the dishes to soak in a tub of water, Kendall put on a pair of clean socks and his sneakers. As he descended the ladder, he sucked in the cool air. Bread baking in the outdoor ovens and pots cooking behind doors gave the air a rich, spicy odor. The village felt close with its narrow streets and two- and three-level adobe homes.

They climbed down the trail and Kendall was amazed he wasn't more sore. His muscles seemed to have relaxed. When he mentioned it, his great-grandfather didn't act surprised.

After a mile, Kendall finally broke the silence. Armando must understand what Kendall's running meant to him. "On the highway, in the truck, it got stronger."

Armando glanced at him, but didn't speak.

Kendall tried to push past the shyness he felt around the elderly man. "I started running a couple years ago because I didn't feel like walking anymore. I had to run. Now I can't stop myself. Everyone calls me the running maniac."

"Running maniac," Armando repeated.

"There's this feeling I get. Like magic. That's what I call it because it's so strong. Like it's whirling all through my arms and legs. I have to run to it. I thought the magic would get weak when we left home, but it didn't. It just got stronger."

"Tell me what happened," his great-grandfather said.

"When we went past Enchanted Mesa, I jumped out and ran." Kendall laughed, knowing his great-grandfather would think he was truly crazy now.

Armando dug his staff into the dirt and stopped. "You jumped out and ran to the mesa," he repeated.

"Uh-huh. The magic took over my legs. I couldn't stop until I touched the rock with my own hands."

"This magic is strong," Armando commented, pulling out his staff and continuing on. When they reached the shale and boulders, the old man stopped and gazed prayerfully at the site as he had done the day before. Then they sat on the rocks to rest.

"Let's have some water." From inside his shirt, Armando pulled out the soft leather pouch that Kendall had seen hanging over the picture. It was round and fat, and Armando laid it on his lap to loosen the strings.

Shining water sparkled inside the leather. When had his great-grandfather filled it and hidden it against his chest?

"I brought this yesterday, but you ran off too soon. Pebbles in the mouth don't help much after a few miles. You almost made yourself sick, boy."

They took turns drinking from the pouch. The deerskin was waterproof and the water cold. After Kendall handed the pouch back, his great-grandfather commanded him to stand.

"Huh?" Kendall grunted.

"Do not say huh," Armando told him, but without sternness. "We obey our elders without asking questions. Especially when they are about to give a gift."

Kendall faced the elderly man, looking into eyes the same chocolate-brown color as his own. Slowly Armando wrapped the deerskin pouch around Kendall's waist, tying the leather straps in a firm knot.

Kendall sucked in his breath. The leather pouch was beautiful, well worn by hands and age. He stroked the softness at his waist, not knowing how to thank this great patriarch. No words sounded right in his head.

"Runners," Armando said, "whether Acoma or not, should not run without water."

Did this mean this elder of Acoma respected his running and trusted him? Even a little?

"And now," his great-grandfather went on, "tell me more about this magical running you seem to possess."

"I don't know what it is. I want to know, but I never seem to make it to where the magic is pulling me. That probably sounds stupid."

"Nothing is foolish if it is a part of you and makes you who you are. Where does it come from? Do you know?"

Kendall shook his head. "It doesn't seem to start or end anywhere."

"Perhaps this magic is circular, with no beginning or end. And perhaps it has always been a part of this world, but only certain people feel it."

Kendall liked that, but it still didn't give any explanations. The ones he wanted.

"Have you ever told anyone this?"

"No, they'd think I was crazy."

"Not even your mother?"

"I tried to tell her about the magic, right before . . . the nurse pulled me away. But I don't think Mom heard me right. The medicine made her talk funny."

"I would like to know what your mother said to you."

"She said—" Kendall shook his head. "It didn't make sense. Dad said she was on painkillers."

"Sometimes we do not understand another's words, especially on their dying bed." Armando stood up to survey the southern ridge of mountains, then looked back at Kendall with a penetrating gaze.

For a moment, Kendall could hear her voice; then it vanished. "She said there is a place that has all the answers."

Abruptly Armando sat down on the rock, leaning heavily against his staff.

"But why did she talk about answers? I hadn't asked her any questions."

"Oh yes you had," his great-grandfather replied. "And she told you all she could say."

9

The water sloshed inside the pouch as Kendall returned to Armando's side. The elderly man's chin seemed to quiver, but perhaps it was the heat of the desert shimmering under the sun.

"You wanted to know where the magic came from," Armando murmured. "You asked your mother why you felt it, what it meant. You knew that she would know."

Kendall let out a shaky breath. His great-grandfather seemed to read his thoughts.

"You are feeling things Acoma people know from the day of their birth. Instincts, like the animals possess." Armando rose and walked out a few steps, pointing to the sky with his staff. "Look at the hawk circling above us in the air. He is the hunter of this valley, my valley. The wind is singing notes across the rocks and sand. The sun is our father, giving warmth and all life. The piñon and sage are my perfume. But you," he said, turning to point his staff at Kendall, "you don't know these things.

"And how can you know? You grew up Anglo. The blood you have—it is almost like it doesn't exist. Your mother gave it to you, but at the same time took it away when she mingled it with another."

The words were spoken quietly, but pierced Kendall right in the center of his soul. But his great-grandfather didn't sound angry, only resigned to something that made him sorrowful.

What was Armando hoping for when he had asked Kendall to come to Acoma? Nothing made much sense if he still resented what his mother had done. And death had stolen his mother's chance to return and make things right between them.

Kendall realized something else: Armando knew what the magic was. It was rooted here at Acoma and in his great-grandfather's past as a runner. The reasons, the explanations he ached for, were all right here. *A place that has all the answers* had to be Acoma. His mother *had* known what he was talking about that day in spite of her illness. Kendall smiled through watery eyes.

He got the sudden crazy urge to call her and tell her, then shook his head at the silliness. It reminded him of a few days after the funeral when he'd arrived home from school and heard a woman's voice in the kitchen. He had sprinted out of his bedroom, not thinking, and called, "Hey, Mom, I'm home. What's for dinner?"

And stopped dead when he saw that it was Mrs. Jenkins, who often brought casseroles those first few weeks. He had wanted to crawl away when he saw the neighbor's surprised, sympathetic face. She pretended she hadn't noticed, rattling on about how to warm the meal in the oven, but Kendall had flown out the door, running to the cottonwood groves by the river to wait until she left.

Brett heard about it and laughed at him later.

So here he was at this place with all the answers. Yet Kendall didn't know where to look. He hadn't made the connection with the strings of magic. Or maybe it was because he didn't know the right questions. He was also afraid that Armando wouldn't want to tell him. Too sacred to share with a stranger, a half-Anglo boy. Kendall still hoped that he had gained a little respect in the old man's eyes with his running, even though he could be stupid about it. Like getting sick and sleeping eighteen hours.

Kendall scrambled over the rocks and looked up at the vertical walls of Enchanted Mesa again.

His great-grandfather moved closer, a puzzled look on his face. "What are you doing, boy?"

"I feel it the strongest at Enchanted Mesa. That's why I must have jumped out of the truck. But it's not crazy and confusing here like it is everywhere else. It's kind of, I don't know. Comforting and powerful all at the same time." Their eyes met and Kendall surprised himself with his next words. "I need to know what it wants me to do. What it wants to show me."

"Perhaps that is the reason you are here," his great-grandfather replied.

"You invited me," Kendall reminded him.

"I did," Armando admitted. "But I didn't know why. I invited you after much prayer and fasting. It was Lydia, your great-grandmother, who kept talking about it, and then Mary who pestered me. I have told you the history of Enchanted Mesa. This place is the beginning of our people. All purposes and destinies lie hidden within its walls. Enchanted Mesa will speak to you *if* there is a destiny here for you."

Kendall wanted to shout out loud. He knew it. He could feel it. "Grandfather," he said, calling him by name for the first time, "how will I know?"

The elderly man leaned forward, studying him carefully.

"No one will have to tell you. When Enchanted Mesa speaks—if she speaks—you will know."

A destiny. The word evoked all kinds of wondrous possibilities. But how could Kendall figure out what it was? And what was he supposed to do?

Armando began the slippery descent to the valley floor, digging his staff into the earth. He turned back. "Do we walk back, or do you run, boy?"

"I'm going to stay here a while longer, then I'm going to run back."

"You have your water now. No more running sickness."

Kendall patted the bag, feeling for that one tiny moment like a runner from a hundred years ago. "Thank you, Grandfather," he said softly.

Armando faced the desert. "We will meet later at home."

Kendall watched the elderly man grow smaller. Armando hadn't admitted that he had been a runner, hadn't told Kendall a single thing about it.

The noise of falling shale shattered the quiet, and Kendall bolted upright. A flash of black disappeared around the southern curve of the mesa.

He was on his feet and running even though his legs still hurt. It had to be the wild horses.

Kendall halted at the curve of the mesa. There they were, two hundred feet ahead of him, nibbling at a patch of grass. His heart crammed into his throat at the sight.

But Rasmiyah was not among them. Kendall wanted to see the white mare so badly. His only hope was to get close enough to touch her. He'd never ridden a horse before in his life, but he wanted so desperately to touch this horse's silky mane and smooth his hands down her warm throat.

Rasmiyah was just like Armando, Kendall realized. Wary. Skittish. In order for him to be accepted at Acoma, both the horse and his great-grandfather had to get to know him.

The only way to do that was to earn their trust and respect. How to do that was a mystery—something he had to figure out.

Squatting on top of the mound of shale, Kendall watched and waited. His foot slipped, and pebbles clattered. The horses raised their big heads and stared at him. Readjusting his balance, Kendall stared back. One by one, the bays and blacks and chestnut-colored horses returned to their chewing.

Kendall became a statue so they wouldn't run off. His feet went numb inside his Nikes. Then his legs tingled in pain.

He shaded his eyes, searching the desert. The most important horse was still missing, but he had to get up. Pretending to be part of the landscape wasn't easy for very long, especially after he stopped being able to feel his legs.

Suddenly, as if she'd been there all along, Rasmiyah trotted around from the far north end of Enchanted Mesa. Kendall rose and fought the urge to run forward, and then the weirdest thing happened. He couldn't move his legs.

They felt like they had turned into a couple of dead tree stumps. Kendall lifted one foot and stamped it. Pain shot downward and he let out a cry.

All the animals stopped their meal, launching glances at him. Kendall heard Rasmiyah grumble in her throat.

The numbness and tingling grew even worse as the circulation returned to his feet. He moaned with the agony, chomping down on his lip to keep from yelling out loud. Kendall felt foolish as the horses watched him with intelligent eyes. Rasmiyah's ears twitched. He had to smile, wondering what they must be thinking about this stone turning into a human.

Testing his legs, Kendall took a step off the shale, trying not to make any sudden moves or to rattle too many rocks.

The instant he stirred, Rasmiyah lifted her feet, dancing

nervously in a circle. The bays and blacks butted each other and moved about restlessly.

Kendall took another few paces, stepping out of the shadow of the mesa and into the sunlight. This bothered the horses even more, and Kendall watched in awe as they pawed the ground.

The lead horse, a black mare with white socks, moved in Kendall's direction, and without hesitation the rest of the herd followed. He watched their trotting turn to galloping.

Suddenly he realized they were headed straight for him. Kendall didn't know whether to run back up into the boulders or stay where he was. Surely the animals wouldn't run up the slope of the rocky mound. Not with an entire desert stretching for miles in all directions. Even so, the pounding hooves coming right for him made Kendall step a few feet closer to Katzima.

Visions of getting trampled ran through his mind. But there were only a dozen or so horses, hardly a herd of buffalos.

The ground began to vibrate. He stood still, though he wanted to flee. The herd picked up speed, leg muscles rippling, nostrils flaring. The numbness was finally gone and Kendall felt a surge of adrenaline in his legs. Without another thought, he turned south and began to run.

Stealing a quick glance backward, Kendall saw they were on his heels, the whole group to his left. Every horse except Rasmiyah.

Kendall whipped his head to the right. There she was, separated from the band and closing in on him.

Perhaps they *were* going to trample him. It was hard not to panic, but he didn't slow down. Instead he picked up speed. If he slowed at all, he'd be caught under their feet for sure.

The sound of galloping horses was deafening. Kendall's

heart slammed against his chest as manes and tails shot by. His legs were going so fast Kendall feared he'd stumble and grind his face into the dirt. To keep from falling, he concentrated on the muscles surging in their rumps, the legs galloping in perfect rhythm, manes flying in the wind.

Rasmiyah was the last. She didn't look at him, but Kendall couldn't help grinning with delight, watching her pass. He was running so fast, he could have sworn he was flying.

The magic was perfect. Running was perfect. As Rasmiyah charged past, Kendall felt her breath rush across his cheeks like a soft, warm breeze.

It lasted for only a moment, but Kendall knew he would remember that moment for the rest of his life.

10

Trina met him at the edge of the cliff as he finished climbing the narrow foot path up to Sky City. "We checked the mail today and you got this."

She handed him two postcards—one from Dad, the other from Brett.

"Thanks," Kendall told her and stuck them in his back pocket.

"They got here fast," Trina commented.

"Huh?"

"You know, you've only been here a few days."

"Oh, yeah."

"Aren't you going to read them?"

Kendall hesitated. He was dying to read them. He just didn't want her looking over his shoulder.

She rolled her eyes. "I promise I won't look. I already read them anyway."

"What!" Kendall flung his arms up in disgust.

Trina stepped back a few paces. "They're only postcards, not letters. Anybody could read them. The mailman, anyone, you know . . ." Her voice trailed off.

"That still doesn't give you the right to read someone else's mail," Kendall told her. His head jerked upward as thunder rumbled. Dry lightning sparked across the black western sky. Dark clouds had moved in fast over the valley.

A single spot of rain hit the pinkish mesa rock, then instantly dried. Kendall waited for another, but it was the only one. He stomped off to be by himself, pulling the postcards out of his pocket only when he was alone.

The first one was a picture of Flagstaff, Arizona, with tall pine trees and a mountain iced with snow. Dad must have bought it the very first day.

Dear Kendall,
    Didn't want you to get homesick right away. Stopped here for burgers and a stamp. Hope everything is okay. I'll write soon. Love, Dad

Kendall ran his finger over the words, noticing his dad's nice handwriting, unlike a typical man's, especially a trucker who never wrote anything but checks for the bills. They'd be in California by now, probably at the beach or Disneyland. He shoved the thoughts away and turned to Brett's card and sloppier penmanship.

Hey, Kiddo,
    Still can't believe you're there and we're here! CA, here we come! Come on, dude, let us come and get you. You don't want to be stuck in that rotten desert all summer, do you? You're crazy, man. But that's nothing we don't already know!
    Brett

Kendall's gut twisted. Part of him wanted to cry with jealousy. Brett always got all the fun with Dad in the truck.

But another part of him wanted to say, "Ha-ha, you're stuck in a truck all summer and I get to look for Mom, who's hiding here. The joke's on you, Brett."

Of course Brett wouldn't buy that in a million years. He'd just laugh at Kendall and know *he* was the lucky one. Kendall jammed the postcards into his rear pocket.

Trina had followed him. She said, "I saw the horses out by Enchanted Mesa. You're not trying to mess with them, are you?"

Kendall shook his head at her persistence. "I would never hurt them, especially not Rasmiyah."

Trina scrutinized him. "You saw her, too?"

Ignoring her question, Kendall headed toward the Abeyta house to distract her from asking any more questions. He didn't want his face to give him away. And he didn't want to end up telling Trina about what had happened by blurting it out just because she was staring at him so darkly.

Running with Rasmiyah on the desert was his own secret.

It was going to rain any second. He was sure of it. Trina followed him, her hair whipping around her mouth in the wind. The sky grew blacker by the second.

"Well, did you?" she persisted.

"Yeah," Kendall admitted, but he didn't add anything else.

"You better remember our deal."

"What deal is that?"

"To stay away from her. Don't you dare try and get close or touch her or ride her or anything!"

Kendall glared at her, resenting her words. Trina didn't understand at all. He would never force Rasmiyah or scare her. The white horse was wary and easily scared off, but she was curious about him, too. They had connected that morning. Kendall felt the power of it.

"It's gonna rain," he finally said. "I'm going home."

"It's not going to rain," Trina contradicted.

"Heck it is. Look at those clouds and that lightning over there."

"Well, you wouldn't know, would you? Because you're not really Acoma."

Kendall stopped. Did they all think that—Trina's mother, her sister? Were they just being polite because they had to? Maybe he'd never belong. Maybe he didn't need to, but he wanted to. Although what that meant, he wasn't really sure.

He took a deep breath to keep from snapping at her. "What are you talking about?"

"It never rains until after the rain dances in July. We offer the spirits and the rain gods our gratitude and we have to show that we're worthy. Everything has to be done in proper order."

Her words sounded so grown-up. Full of things he knew nothing about.

"It never rains here at Acoma until after the rain dances?" he asked.

"That's right."

"What do the dancers do to make it rain?"

"I can't tell you. The ceremonies are too sacred. A lot of them I don't even know because the men perform them in the kivas."

"Will I be able to go?" Kendall asked cautiously.

Trina shook her head and laughed. "Not into the kiva!"

"Why?"

"Three reasons. Three *big* reasons." Trina ticked them off on her fingers. "You're not a registered member of the tribe. You're not initiated into a society. Plus your dad is—"

"I *know*," Kendall cut her off. He knew what his father was, and he knew what his father wasn't. And neither was good or bad in itself. He hated feeling as though everybody was staring at him because he had Anglo blood. He'd been

76

raised by an Anglo father that he loved. And he yearned for his Acoma mother because he loved her, too. Kendall felt like he had to straddle a thin line, two ways of living and believing, and neither one seemed easy.

11

Every day Kendall got up at dawn to run to Enchanted Mesa. He filled the leather pouch with water and strapped it to his waist. After a week he could run all the way without stopping once. Once he arrived, he ran around the entire mesa, watching Katzima until it seemed as though he had every crevice and color memorized.

Enchanted Mesa remained quiet about its secrets. Perhaps it had none, or perhaps they were locked away from boys who weren't really Acoma. But every morning the cords curled around his body and tugged him across the desert.

Every afternoon black clouds rolled in to hover over Sky City. Tourists scurried to find shelter near the flat walls of the homes or inside the church, deceived by the ominous sky.

Inside the pueblo, Kendall watched thunder rattle the cups on the table. Hot white flashes crackled overhead. But it didn't rain. The moisture never made it to the earth, halted as if the rain itself knew it wasn't time. He'd never seen such a thing. And the magic intensified.

He once heard Mary, out by her pottery table, whisper, "The gods are playing with us."

One morning Kendall woke to the sounds of his great-grandfather moving about in the dark kitchen. He got up to find a shirt, and a moment later Armando was next to him, holding a bowl of water.

The elderly man held up a hand to stop Kendall from dressing. He sank back onto his sleeping bag as his great-grandfather kindled a fire on the small hearth. The shadows from the flickering yellow flames danced against the ceiling like sunlight.

Armando beckoned Kendall to rise. Then the elder knelt in front him. "Today we will prepare you for the running." Ceremoniously, Armando took a cloth, soaked it in the bowl of water sprinkled with herbs, and began to wash Kendall's legs. His great-grandfather repeated words in Keresan that Kendall couldn't understand as he bathed Kendall's arms, legs, and shoulders.

After a few minutes he began to speak to Kendall in English. "Rebecca, your mother, was beautiful and bright," his great-grandfather said, rinsing Kendall's feet. "She helped her grandmother bake bread in the outdoor ovens and cook the meals. She carried the *tinajas*, the water jars, from the cisterns. Keeping Old Acoma the way it has always been for centuries helps us maintain our traditions, our religion, our way of life. Other tribes may install water and electric lights into their adobe homes, but it is artificial. We do not advance with the times, as they say. We are timeless."

Kendall felt the power pulling at him. Armando's rich voice was like magic itself. He wished his mother could be here, too, in this place she loved and never saw again. He'd been hoping for this moment when his great-grandfather would tell him about her and talk to him just as he was doing now.

His great-grandfather picked up a branch of hemlock,

swished it in the herbs, and rubbed Kendall's skin until it burned. He wanted to burst out the door and run across the valley. He could run that far; he knew it. At that moment he felt as if he could do anything.

Picking up a small bowl, Armando carefully dipped a finger into it, stirring the paste inside. With his forefinger, he smeared a white streak up Kendall's arms from his wrists to his elbows, zigzagging the paint in a design like a snake.

"This symbol represents our clan. All runners paint their clan symbol. I will not do all your body—that is for ceremonies—but today you need to know the way of the runners. For weeks you have proved to me the love you have for running and the talent you possess. Today, you don't have to run alone. The gods will be with you."

Armando picked up a bundle from the table and led Kendall outside. They climbed a second ladder that led to the roof. On top of the house, they were higher than the entire village. Kendall felt as if he and Armando were the only two people alive at that moment, looking out over the sacred world the gods had made for them. One by one stars winked out, but it was still dark—the dark before the dawn.

His great-grandfather raised his voice and arms upward and began to pray to the Sky Chief. When he was finished, he turned to Kendall and translated the words. "I pray for your health and spiritual strength, the strength to become who you are meant to become and the courage to make the choices you will have to make. All tribes have had to endure suffering and death. Most painful is the pain of change, the loss of our ways. But suffering, death, even change means nothing, because I have endured with the things I loved most. I was able to have them because of those that went before me.

"It is because I am Acoma. I am connected with the earth, with the gods, with all that is beautiful. Today I am at peace with you, my son, Kendall. But you—perhaps you have the harder lot. You are both Acoma and Anglo. At the same time you are neither. There is a long road ahead of you to find out who you are. The journey on that road is never easy."

Armando bent to unfold the bundle he had brought with him. He picked up a leather skirt-like garment and tied it around Kendall's waist. "Your feet are soft and tender from shoes, so I will allow you to wear these," he told him, and helped Kendall put on boots that resembled moccasins.

His great-grandfather straightened and the two locked eyes. Wearing the runner's clothing and the clan symbol of lightning, Kendall felt as if he had become a different person. Or perhaps his real self was emerging. He breathed deeply with the joy of the feeling, then realized that his great-grandfather had stopped.

An odd expression flickered across the elderly man's face. He looked reflective, less solemn. "This morning you are like me when I was twelve. For a moment we have traded places. You have become me as a boy and I have become my own grandfather preparing me for the running. I was born Deer Clan and ran before I could walk. I became the swiftest runner of the pueblo. When I married my wife, who was Snake Clan, I was adopted to help carry on the runner traditions that had already died with the men of that clan. Too many clans have disappeared."

"I will run my best for you," Kendall told him.

"No." His great-grandfather shook his head. "Run your best for yourself and the gods. If you do that, all will be well." He reached down for the last parcel and opened it for Kendall to see the various items. "I have prepared your sacred bundle to carry when you run. A prayer stick with eagle feathers to give your prayers wings to fly to the gods and Iatiku, our mother. Herbs for strength and health. Here is a snake carved from piñon to remind you of your heritage in the Snake Clan and your purpose. Also, there is a tiny perfect ear of white corn, most sacred. Iatiku gave us the gift of corn to make our bread and give us life."

He tied the small leather bundle to Kendall's waist, then put a necklace strung with a single turquoise stone around his neck. "This stone will give you health. It is the stone that stole its color from the sky."

Kendall pictured the strands of turquoise his mother liked to wear. That image was all he could conjure up, just her hands with their rings and bracelets. Now he and she wore the same stone.

"Now," Armando commanded, placing his hands on Kendall's shoulders, "you are ready to run with all your heart."

Kendall had a sudden memory of those same words. His mother had told him something like that once. He strained to remember, but the memory was gone as fast as it had come.

"Grandfather," Kendall said boldly, "what direction did you run when you were a runner?"

The old man didn't even blink. This was the first time Kendall had asked him about his running. "I was the runner for the south," he replied.

"How far did you have to run?"

"Some years many miles, some years fewer," he answered. "It was a matter of purification. We ran until we felt the gods had listened to our prayers for water. We ran and the dancers danced. And the rain came. It has been many generations since the ancient runners."

Kendall held his breath.

"Only the Snake Clan remembers the old way," his great-grandfather said, tying the sacred bundle around Kendall in a firm square knot. "Back in the time of the ancients all the pueblo tribes performed the Snake Dance, but today the only tribe with a full Snake Clan is the Hopis. They still perform the Snake Dance, but it has been many years since I could travel to their three mesas to watch. At Acoma the Snake Clan has been too small for many generations, and I never performed it myself. I only carry the memories of past runners."

The Snake Dance. Kendall shivered in the dawn air. The magic tugged at his toes and ankles, making him want to jump down the ladder and run, but he waited for the moment when Armando would release him to the desert.

Snakes. Lightning. Zigzags. Summer rain. It seemed impossible, unreal. But Kendall knew there was power there somewhere in the snakes and the gods, power connected to the ancient times. Connected in ways nobody but Armando knew anymore.

"Tell me about the runners and the Snake Dance. What did they do?"

"I cannot tell you yet. But one day the time will be right."

"Then what do the clans do now to bring rain?"

"There are kachinas and rain dances and footraces. We perform our stories and dances in the kivas. And the gods hear us and bless Acoma Valley with the rain."

"And the rain comes?"

"The rain always comes," his great-grandfather assured him.

Kendall felt dizzy with the memories passed down from clansmen before him. And the magic—the power of the snakes—knew who he was.

12

Kendall climbed down the ladder and jogged through the quiet village. When he reached the cliff trail and descended, he began to run. The air was cold on his bare chest, but the shoes were comfortable.

It felt new and strange to run with leather flapping against his thighs and bundles tied to his front and back waist. But they were comforting, as if his great-grandfather and those who had run before were beside him.

With a prayer stick in the shape of a snake, cornmeal for purification, and strength from the stone, Kendall ran as he never had before. Gliding across stones and brush, he was part of the cactus, part of the sand, part of the wind itself.

When he was in the desert, he had fleeting moments when his uncertainty dissolved, when he felt as if he was beginning to belong. Perhaps because the valley belonged to him alone at these solitary times. There was no one to tell him he wasn't Acoma.

Kendall breathed in and out, legs strong, arms pumping. Days of hot sun were turning his skin even darker. He hadn't had a haircut in months. Dad often forgot, and now

Kendall's hair fell below his ears and swept his neck, tickling him as he ran. He wanted to grow it long like Armando's and tie it back in leather and braids.

He pushed at his red bandanna, wiping at the dripping sweat.

A blaze of golden sun shot over the edge of the mountains. In the mornings, running east, sunlight always blinded him.

Today the sky was turquoise like the stone around his neck. Pearly dawn unfolded over Enchanted Mesa. He ached for her to give him a sign, to speak, to do something. Throw a rock at him, even, but finally notice that he was here for his answers. He was ready for the answers. What more was there for him to do?

The mesa stood as it had since the beginning of creation, silent and serene. She was too magnificent to talk to him. And when would he become pure enough?

Kendall untied his bundle and held the carved snake in his hands. He could tell it was old: it was worn smooth with age, the snake's red zigzags fading. Underneath the ear of white corn, he found feathers and a pocketknife tucked into the bottom of the bundle.

It was time to make his own prayer stick as Armando had shown him during the long summer evenings.

He scoured the surrounding brush until he found a piñon bush, from which he broke off a branch. Sitting down on a flat stone, Kendall began to whittle and polish the wood. It took a long time to get it right. When he was satisfied, he carefully cut notches and tied the feathers to the stick. At last he walked to the far east side of Katzima, and paused for a moment of silence. Then he climbed, using the indentations in the walls to help raise himself higher. Not too far up, he found a deep crevice in the side of the rock, and there he placed the prayer stick.

It wasn't much, but it was a beginning. Perhaps the spirits would know he existed now.

He returned to the wide smooth boulder to wait for Rasmiyah. It wasn't too long before she appeared with her wild herd, kicking up clouds of dirt. Most of the horses raced past, not even seeing Kendall. Rasmiyah slowed to look at him, but today she didn't stop.

Over the last weeks or so she had often pranced near. Kendall would stand as still as he could. After several minutes, he would hold out his hand, palm up.

She would snort, seeming to want to try his touch. Then suddenly she'd shy away, kicking up her heels like a flirt.

Kendall grew hungry and it was growing hotter. It was time to get going. He headed back home, after a final glance at the spot where the prayer stick lay safe.

About a mile across the sand, Kendall suddenly gasped as Rasmiyah tore past him out of nowhere. He hadn't heard her coming up behind him.

"Hey," he said, as startled as if he'd been ambushed. He tried to keep his pace and not scare her by stopping suddenly. As he ran, she darted back and forth, at first several yards away, then closing in until only a few feet separated them.

Kendall grinned.

She shook her mane and slowed until her running matched his. Kendall held both arms out wide and kept his speed. It was hard, but he kept his arms out, wondering what the white horse would do. "Where are your friends?" he asked.

Rasmiyah just grunted deep in her throat and rolled her eyes.

Kendall lost sight of her when she suddenly put on the brakes and fell behind. It was tempting to stop also, but he didn't want to scare her. Kendall kept running, arms aching.

This time he heard Rasmiyah pounding behind him. Then they were side by side with only a foot separating them. Kendall felt her mane tickle his outstretched hands. He wiggled his fingers in the softness, still running and wondering if he'd fall right over, he was going so fast.

She snorted and Kendall could feel her breath in his palm. He was like an eagle skimming the sand, wings wide. He had become a part of the desert, one of the animals.

A moment later, Rasmiyah sped up and cut in front of him, galloping off to the south.

"Aah!" Kendall cried, letting out a whoop of joy. If she hadn't been so fast he might have tripped over her when she thundered past. It was scary to think about falling under her powerful legs, but she had timed it so as not to hurt him.

And today she had let him touch her.

13

Kendall was dragging by the time he arrived back at Sky City, but the delight of finally being able to touch Rasmiyah was like a tickle of joy that kept bubbling up. Dressed only in leather and half naked besides, Kendall avoided the early tourist groups until he reached the Abeyta house.

He took off his water pouch and the bundle and laid them next to the hearth, then dressed in shorts and a T-shirt, folding the leather apron and moccasins inside a blanket. In the kitchen, Kendall poured a bowl of chicken and green chili stew, cut a slice of bread, then sat down. He went through the stack of mail sitting on one end of the table, looking for a postcard from Dad. The last one had been from Tampa, Florida.

Gulf water 85 degrees. Great body surfing. Gonna take you back here for shrimp and a boogie board in August.

There was a letter today. Kendall stopped chewing and studied the envelope. The postmark was smeared, but the front of the envelope was stained with grease. Some café somewhere. Kendall could almost smell meat sizzling on the grill and coffee brewing.

Dear Son,

Got tired of picking out fancy postcards for you. I just had to write. My timing may not be very good, and you know I'm pretty mushy when it comes to stuff like this, but I'm missing you something terrible. It's been a month, and this truck cab is getting to be the loneliest place in the world even with Brett talking my right ear off.

We gab with other truckers on the CB, and there are some pretty nice truck stops with good food and showers and all, but it just isn't the same without both my boys sitting next to me.

You know I wouldn't even be doing this if it didn't have a better salary than my local stuff. But I'm not saying anything you don't already know. I've found out that I'm not cut out for the long hauling. Gotta come home to my baby. (Sorry to be such a wimp.)

Here's the long and the short of it—I can't wait another three weeks to see you. On our way back west before we head north, I want to pick you up. It's a short summer and we're spending too much of it apart. Our first one without Mom should be together. Call me on the radio through the dispatcher. That's the number I put inside the pocket of your duffel.

I can't wait to see you!
Love, Dad

Kendall refolded the letter and slipped it back into the envelope. A couple of weeks ago he would have been glad to go, even anxious. He'd felt awkward, out of place, and out of sorts, counting the days.

But things had changed. For him and for his great-grandfather. He had agreed to come to Acoma because of the possibility that his mother was in this place where the spirits lived and the gods ruled. But there hadn't been a sign of her. Not a single one. It was as if she didn't exist. But the magic got him here in the first place, and the magic compelled him to stay now.

Whatever he had thought was in store for him hadn't happened. Enchanted Mesa might be just a big chunk of white stone plunked down on the desert and nothing else.

Even as the thought crossed his mind, Kendall knew it wasn't true. The magic was alive there, a spirit that urged him forward. He had to be getting closer to finding his mother. There were signs. Kendall could feel the bond between Armando and him growing. He was learning about Acoma, even learning Keresan words and phrases. All that was left was to make the connection with his mother. To find her through the power of the ancient magic. Giving up and going home meant that he'd be turning his back on the chance to see her once more.

Kendall dipped his spoon into his bowl again. Suddenly his great-grandfather stood at his shoulder. The elderly man knew a letter had arrived, but he didn't say a word, just poured himself a bowl of soup and broke bread into it.

They ate in silence and Kendall finally said, "My dad told me once that Mom's real self isn't in a grave, that she's somewhere else. He doesn't know where, but he knows she's not completely gone. Do you think that's true?"

Armando's white hair brushed the table edge. "Your father is right. There is no death."

"No death? How can that be?"

"Death is not the end of the spirit. What we call death is really only a change of worlds."

Kendall liked that. It echoed what Dad had always said.

But if Mom was still around, why couldn't he feel her? Why did she seem to have ceased to exist?

"This land is filled with the invisible dead of Acoma," his great-grandfather went on. "It is populated by the spirits of those we cannot see. They live in the mountains and the valleys and in the very sand and brush around us."

"Then why can't I remember her anymore?" Kendall let his spoon drop, swiping at his eyes and feeling embarrassed.

Armando nodded slowly, watching him. "It is what I thought. You want your mother back. That first week you weren't happy. I wondered how a boy like you had agreed to come."

Kendall fingered the letter and didn't know what to do. Dad was probably already on his way back to New Mexico.

"You can feel your mother," his great-grandfather went on. "Because she is in the magic. She gave you a gift passed through her blood. This magic ties you to Enchanted Mesa and the people of Acoma."

Armando Abeyta set his face more firmly as if to keep his own emotions in control, but his voice gave him away. "I thought she had lost her Acoma ways when she left, but the magic of the Snake Clan has come back to me through you, Kendall. When the time is right, I believe you will have her again."

"Can I really be a part of the Snake Clan? Will you tell me about the Snake Dance of the ancients?"

His great-grandfather didn't answer his questions, said only, "Keep running. Never stop running. There will be answers in it."

"But what about the clan?" Kendall asked again, knowing he shouldn't be so persistent. His need to know, to begin, was so urgent.

Armando smiled. "When the time is right I will tell you the memories I hold of our ancient clan."

Kendall slowly finished his bread. Then his great-grandfather laid a leathery hand on his arm. "Tell me what has come from your father."

"Dad wants to come pick me up."

"That is what I suspected."

"Not because he thinks—" Kendall started. "He says our family shouldn't be apart."

"I can understand that."

"What should I do?" Kendall asked.

His great-grandfather shook his head. "No one can tell you what to do. It is your own decision."

"Is there a place where I can call him?"

"We'll find Mary and borrow her truck."

Kendall followed Armando down the ladder and they walked around the rows of homes until they reached the Ramirezes' table. Tourists were picking up the pottery bowls and animal figurines, checking the prices on the stickers attached to the bottom of each piece.

Trina finished helping a customer, then came around the table. "Hi."

"Hi."

"You want a soda pop? We have some in the ice chest under the table."

The afternoon was heating up. Under the hot sun everybody looked sweaty. Trina kneeled down and pulled out a small cooler filled with cans of soda. She handed him a root beer and took one for herself. "That'll be fifty cents," she said.

Kendall had already snapped the tab. "Huh?"

"Just kidding. You're so gullible. In the summertime we do sell soda, but we haven't made it to the store to restock, so there's only enough for us today."

Trina's older sister, Corinne, had taken over the customers while their mother and Armando went down the road for a moment together.

"I saw you," Trina said, staring at Kendall.

"Huh? Saw me when?"

"Earlier. When you got back from your running. You were sneaking around all decked out."

"I was, huh?"

"You can never be an Acoma runner or dancer, you know," Trina told him. "If that's what you're practicing for."

"Why not?" Kendall asked, without admitting anything.

"Because you don't know about it. You haven't been initiated into a kiva or trained. I hope you didn't just try on some of Great-uncle's things."

Kendall gripped the soda. He wanted to snap at her. How could Trina assume he would use things without permission? "Maybe it wasn't even me."

"Who else has been running around here?" Trina said, as if it were painfully obvious.

"I think the heat's getting to you. You're imagining things."

"Oh, right. Like I'm going to imagine you dressed as someone from a hundred years ago with a water pouch climbing over the edge of the cliff."

"Stranger things have happened," Kendall said in a serious voice. "Maybe you saw a spirit warrior from long ago and thought it was me. You know, people don't really die. They only change worlds, and they can come back in visions and dreams."

"I know that!" Trina huffed, and Kendall knew he was starting to bug her like she bugged him. But he'd never tell her about the special ceremony he and his great-grandfather had shared that morning. It was too special—sacred, even, and private. It angered him that she believed she knew everything and could tell him what to do.

"Watch out, Trina, you never know when you're going to run into a dead person climbing over the cliff," Kendall couldn't help saying.

"You're really annoying, you know that!"

"*I'm* annoying? I'm not the one spying and ordering people around. Or telling certain people to stay away from certain horses that don't even belong to them."

"She belongs to me more than she belongs to you!"

Suddenly his great-grandfather stepped between them.

Kendall shut his mouth. Trina lowered her face.

Armando Abeyta's voice was terribly quiet. "No more arguing. We do not ask our young men about their ceremonial preparations, and we leave wild horses as they are. On the desert—wild. We will respect their freedom."

"Yes, sir," Kendall said.

Trina mumbled something and returned to the pottery table.

"It's time to go," Armando said.

Mary had left her truck parked near the road. Armando stuck the key into the ignition while Kendall climbed in the passenger seat. They drove down the hill to the pay phones at the visitor's center.

Kendall dug out the number for the company dispatcher and put the call through, charging it to the phone card Dad had given him. He'd never used it before, but the operator helped him.

In a few minutes, Dad's voice crackled over the receiver. "Hey, buddy, it's good to hear you!"

Kendall couldn't stop the grin from spreading across his face when he heard his father's voice. "Hi, Dad. I miss you."

"Did you get all my postcards?"

"Yeah. Where are you?"

"Corpus Christi and heading your way. It'll be day after tomorrow before I see you. Texas is huge—takes more than a day to drive across. Hey, did my letter arrive?"

"Yeah. Just today."

"So, what do you think? Great idea, huh? I can't wait to see you."

"I can't wait to see you, too."

Dad let out a huge sigh of relief. "I've been wanting to hear you say that."

Kendall thought about how badly he wanted to see his dad. Every night he'd counted the days until Dad returned for him. But some time during the last week, he'd stopped counting. The rest of the world seemed to have faded away.

Armando had been standing in the sun a few paces away, arms crossed, watching Kendall's face. Now he turned his back and walked down the sidewalk.

His great-grandfather's retreating figure did something strange to Kendall's heart. He cleared his throat. "I wish I could see you, too," he said, reversing what he'd just said.

It took a minute for his words to register.

"What? What did you say, son? This connection must be bad."

Kendall could hear his father tapping the receiver; he swallowed hard. "What I meant to say was, you'd better not stop. I can't leave, Dad. Not yet."

"Kendall." The hurt in his father's voice was painful, and Kendall heard him sniff. "What's up? Something wrong?"

"Oh no, nothing's wrong at all."

"Well, that's good. Have you decided you like it there? More than home?" Dad said it like he was kidding, but the nervous laugh gave him away.

"Dad, come on. I'm not planning on staying here permanently. You know that."

"You had me worried there for a second, good buddy."

"There's still some stuff I have to do here. Please, it's important. I can't go home yet. I didn't think this would happen. I really didn't."

"Well, I didn't expect it, either," Dad said, surrender in his voice. "I just assumed you'd be happy to let me get you. Even Brett misses you!"

Kendall tried to laugh. Brett would never understand what was happening here at Acoma. "I still want to go on our trip together like we'd planned."

"What's going on out there? What is it you've got to do?"

"Can I tell you later? It's hard to explain."

"Sure," Dad said, sighing. "I guess I can wait. I guess I have to. But you're positive everything's okay?"

"Positive. I promise."

"I still don't think I can wait three more weeks. I want to come in a week. That's the longest I can hold out."

A week! It wasn't much time, Kendall knew. It would have to be enough, though, and at least he wouldn't miss the rain ceremonies, if they included him.

"We'd better sign off," Dad finally said.

"Ten-four," Kendall blurted out, trying to cheer him up.

"I love you," his father said, choking up again.

"I love you, too."

"Keep in touch," Dad added.

"Bye, Dad."

Kendall hung up. He felt as though he'd hurt his father's feelings, and it was hard not to feel guilty.

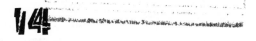

14

Kendall and Armando didn't talk much while they went through the evening preparations for dinner. As they cooked, thunder rattled the screen door as if someone were trying to come in. Wind howled down the stovepipe and dry lightning flashed like white-hot sparks.

After eating and washing up, Armando went to his bedroom and returned, holding a packet of papers in his hands. "I have been thinking about your father, and how hard it was to tell him you wanted to stay."

He sat on the hard adobe seat against the wall. "There is an old story about Ka-sa-wa-te, a father from long ago that I want to tell you. In the early days of the people there was a terrible creature with wings of flint and huge, sharp claws. He was called Flint Bird, and he kidnapped people to his home in the sky far away."

"He sounds scary," Kendall said, lying back on his sleeping bag, the pillow bunched under his head.

"One day, soon after Ka-sa-wa-te's wife died, Flint Bird stole his only son. Because of his wife's death, their son was doubly precious to Ka-sa-wa-te, and he grieved terribly.

Immediately he went in search of his son. When he found Flint Bird's home, the monstrous bird put Ka-sa-wa-te through many ordeals, telling him that if he passed the tests he would get his son back."

"What kind of tests did he have to do?"

"First, Flint Bird caused a mighty hailstorm and blasts of freezing wind to howl up from the pond to kill Ka-sa-wa-te, but Spider Boy helped him and spun a web to cover and protect the warrior and keep him warm. In the morning, Flint Bird was surprised to see Ka-sa-wa-te still alive. So he told him to chop all the weeds from the cornfields before the sun set. It was an impossible task—the cornfields stretched for miles. Spider Boy helped him again by spinning a huge web over the entire field and pulling up all the weeds. Flint Bird was so angry, he told Ka-sa-wa-te to harvest all the corn, build an oven large enough to roast it, and cut enough wood to heat it. All before the sun set."

"That's impossible!" Kendall couldn't help exclaiming.

His great-grandfather smiled. "It is not impossible when you have the animals and the gods to help you. Ka-sa-wa-te had proved his kindness and good heart, so Spider Boy and his friends the Badgers helped him harvest the corn, cut the firewood, and build the oven.

"Of course, Flint Bird became very angry and pushed Ka-sa-wa-te into the oven to burn. Flint Bird thought he had won, but Ka-sa-wa-te was prepared. He had already exchanged Flint Bird's stony wings for pitch-covered ones and wore the stone wings himself. Ka-sa-wa-te was protected and Flint Bird was not. The fiery blast was so hot that soon Flint Bird himself was dead from the heat and flames."

Kendall stared into their own fire at the end of the story, picturing his mother as a child sitting at this same hearth, hearing the same story.

His great-grandfather said, "Ka-sa-wa-te's love for his

son reminds me of the love your father has for you. He wants to protect you and do what is best."

"But he doesn't think you're Flint Bird," Kendall burst out.

Armando laughed. "I know that. This story is just an example. I tell you this as a way to show my grudges and bad feelings are disappearing. It is time they were gone. I don't know when my life will be over, but I need to leave this world with a healed heart. And now it is time for a more recent story. One about you, Kendall."

Kendall got up on his knees and drew closer. "What do you mean?"

"It is time to show you the letter your mother wrote to me a few months before she died."

Kendall had no idea what he was talking about.

"The letter she wrote is about you."

"What did she say?"

"As you know, it was not my idea to have you come to Acoma and visit."

Was this another example of how Armando didn't want him? For a fleeting moment, Kendall wished he were with Dad and Brett in the truck far away on Highway 40, not here with his great-grandfather studying him.

"I see your thoughts," the elderly man said.

Kendall shifted on his blanket and ducked his head.

"You have no reason to feel ashamed, boy. Your mother knew about your running. She knew what you felt."

Kendall's head shot up. "But how could she? I never got a chance to tell her."

"Remember that your mother is Snake Clan. She knew you. You were close to her, yes?"

Kendall nodded, longing sweeping over him.

"Even though she was sick, she was aware of the power-ful spirits you felt in your running, and she wanted to tell me. She knew how important it was. Your mother asked me if you could come."

"I didn't know she'd written to you and asked. She never told me."

Armando held up a sheet of blue stationery and Kendall recognized it from the supply his mother had kept in her desk at home. "It took a year to honor her request, but this is part of the letter she wrote to me. I want you to read it."

Kendall took the worn, crumpled sheet from his great-grandfather. It was obviously a letter that had been handled and read often.

I know I took my sons from you when I married Reid, but he was the man I loved, and I couldn't keep myself from him. Brett, our oldest, is very much like his father, but Kendall—he has just turned eleven, and he is different.

You may not believe this, but Kendall is you, Grandfather, all over again, three generations later. He runs, and he doesn't know why he runs, but I know he feels something special when he's running. It is the spirit of our clan, of Acoma, but he doesn't know that yet. He doesn't know how to name what he feels. I weep with joy to see him following in the Snake Clan's footsteps. Please, my father, you are the one who raised me. Can you find it in your heart to forgive me and know your great-grandson? Kendall needs you. I only have a few weeks left, and if Kendall can't have me, I want him to have you. This is important to me, and I know Reid will not keep him from visiting you. Reid is a good man, he really is . . .

When Kendall looked up, he noticed the suggestion of tears across his great-grandfather's lined cheeks, but the man's face was impassive.

"It took my wife's death to get me past my stubbornness," Armando admitted. "And Mary's nagging. I expected a spoiled Anglo boy to come. And I was surprised." He held out a small envelope. "This came with the letter. It's from your mother and she wanted me to give it to you when you arrived. I've had it for over a year now, but it belongs to you."

Kendall swallowed hard as he took the envelope. The letter was his mother speaking from her deathbed—speaking to him.

"I will go to bed so you can read it in private." His great-grandfather straightened his back and grasped the walking stick to help himself up. All of a sudden he looked very old and frail. "Before I leave, I must tell you that your mother was right, and I'm glad you have come."

Kendall clutched the letter, speechless, anxious to read it. But hearing his great-grandfather's words made tears burn his eyes.

Armando walked to the door of his room, then turned back. "Come here, Grandson."

It was the first time his great-grandfather had called him that, and Kendall liked how it sounded in Armando's deep voice. He scrambled to his feet and went to stand before him.

"I know it was hard to tell your father, but I am glad you will stay for a little longer. I have my own preparations to make before I leave this world and enter the next."

Kendall felt an alarm go off inside his head. "You're not sick, are you?"

"Absolutely not," Armando replied. "How many ninety-five-year-old men do you know who walk six miles a day?"

Kendall gave him a smile. "Only one."

"A spirit might be immortal, but a body is not. I may live ten more years or I may live only ten more days. But I am strong enough to make my annual journey to the sacred shrine."

"When are you leaving?"

"Early in the morning. It is many miles, so I will be gone two days. One day to reach the shrine. After I spend the night there, it will take another day to walk home."

"What will I do while you're gone?"

"You will run, of course. And Mary will keep you and Trina busy. Read your letter now and see what last words your mother wishes to tell you."

"Good night," Kendall said as the old man closed the door to his room. Hurrying back to his sleeping bag, he tore the letter open with shaking hands.

Dearest Son,

At last you are at Acoma! Not together as we planned, but you have journeyed alone and you've made it. I try to picture you older, taller, maturing into a young man, and it's hard to write this knowing I cannot watch you grow. What I would give to be with you in the pueblo, sitting by the hearth, watching you prepare for running and the ceremonies.

I hope you know the reasons for the running—the power you feel—and the strength it can give you. Since you were a little boy, I knew you were Acoma, my grandfather reborn, and I relived my own memories and love for my home through our stories and time together. I always missed Acoma and my family, but I can leave this world a little easier and go to the next knowing you will soon be in my beloved home again.

And Kendall, I am there. I am with you. I will always be with you. If you are at Acoma, then I am beside you, holding you in spirit and always loving you.

Kendall stared into the dim corners of the room, straining to see his mother's face, to hear her voice. Surely the letter would bring her back. It was her paper, her handwriting, her smell fading from the page, but he heard nothing, saw nothing.

Burying his face into the pillow, he fell asleep, clutching the letter.

It was storming last August when he had run home after the first week of school. As he ran, thunder grumbled so fiercely it was like a giant shaking the sky. Rain turned into instant puddles on the dusty ground. Dad had just gotten back from a quick two-day haul to Denver. The doctor was trying some new medicine.

When he got inside the door, Kendall started to strip off his wet clothes. "Hey, Mom," he had called.

Just then an ambulance pulled up into the driveway, siren screaming.

Dad rushed into the front hall, almost knocking Kendall off his feet. "She's gone," he choked when the attendants charged in the door like an army.

The storm had taken his mother.

Kendall and his mother had loved summer storms. They watched them all during July and August while they waited for Dad and Brett to come home between their trips. They sat on the back porch and counted lightning bolts, eating bowls of chocolate chip ice cream.

It always made him wonder if the rain god Strongteeth had stolen his mother. Kidnapped her and taken her someplace that no one knew about. It was just like the story his mother used to tell him about Strongteeth stealing Blue Water and her son. But this time Strongteeth left the son behind.

Kendall never saw her again. Dad wouldn't let him go to the mortuary, and the casket had been closed at the funeral.

*   *   *

Kendall woke with a start and sat up in his underwear. He was sweaty and shaking from the dream. "Grandfather?" He could hear him rustling in the kitchen.

He felt Armando's warm, knotted hands take his. "Hey, hey, hey," came the deep voice. "You were thrashing about, Grandson. Are you ill?"

"Just the dream about the rain god, Strongteeth."

"You mother told you the story about Strongteeth and Blue Water?" There was surprise in his great-grandfather's voice.

"She told me lots of stories before she got sick. But she died during the storm and I thought Strongteeth had stolen her. Red and blue and white lightning bolts shot down from the sky, just like Strongteeth's arrows."

"Sometimes there are answers in dreams."

"I only dream about the day Mom died. There aren't any signs or answers."

"All dreams have messages. Listen closely for yours. The gods send them to us for a reason."

It was comfortable in the darkness, easier to talk.

"I was thinking about how Blue Water is my mother's story, and Flint Bird is my father's. What story is there for me?"

"I think you will write your own story. But if I were to give you a story or a name right now, I would say that someday people might call you the Boy Who Raced the Horse."

Kendall took a sharp breath. Armando had seen him with Rasmiyah, then. The elderly man seemed to know everything.

"Go back to sleep now. It is the middle of the night. I won't see you for two days. I'm leaving for the sacred shrine. I want to walk while the air is cool, and it is a long way."

Kendall sat up higher and realized his great-grandfather was wearing long leather breeches and an embroidered shirt. His white hair was braided and pulled back with the bandanna. Heavy silver and turquoise necklaces decorated his chest. A sacred bundle was tied at his waist, along with a string of small bells.

"I'll go with you," Kendall said, wanting to make the journey at his great-grandfather's side.

"No, this journey is my personal one of purification before the rain ceremonies begin."

"I'd like to run with you sometime."

Armando smiled. "I won't be running, Grandson, only walking. Next year you will be ready to go with me."

"When will you be back?"

"Late tomorrow afternoon. We'll have supper together tomorrow night."

15

Kendall couldn't sleep after Armando left. He got up, bathed with herb water, and prepared himself for the run to Enchanted Mesa. When he reached the great spire, the air was motionless and heavy with fat clouds. He sat on the rocks, listening to faraway thunder that rumbled like an old woman.

Kendall had a sense of freedom, of long lazy hours ahead. No rush to get back for lunch. He threw rocks to see how far they would skitter across the sand, then looked for more places to climb the mesa. There weren't many, and the few hand and footholds ended ten feet or so up the sheer sides.

He hung around, hoping for Rasmiyah's appearance, but there was no sign of the herd on the horizon of wavering hot sand.

When the sun was high in the sky, Kendall began to jog back. Rasmiyah must be miles away. It was rare not to see her, if only from a distance.

Kendall had gone about half a mile when something nipped his shoulder. He whirled, muscles tense. Not five feet away, Rasmiyah stood, pawing the ground.

"Hey!" Kendall cried. "You bit me!"

The white horse lifted her head, snorting, then shook it from side to side. She danced in place as if she couldn't keep still.

"You're a sneaky thing to bite me like that."

Kendall didn't move any closer, not wanting her to go tearing off. Except for when she had breathed into his palm and raced away, Kendall had never been this close to her.

She was beautiful, smooth and white. Not a tall animal, but perfectly his size. Her tail arched high, and her eyes were black and wide and clear.

Rasmiyah continued to shake her head at him and stamp the ground. Kendall knew she wanted to come closer, but it was a daring step for a wild horse.

"I can wait as long as you can," Kendall said quietly. He'd wait like a rock. He was getting good at that. Or maybe he'd become the wind, moving but invisible.

She circled him, closing in, but Kendall didn't even turn his head. Rasmiyah nibbled him on the arm again, but not as hard this time.

"You silly girl. See, you can bite me all you want and I won't jump or yell."

The white horse nickered and Kendall felt her breath on his face. She stepped closer, and as slowly as he could, he lifted a hand to stroke her forelock. Her sun-warmed coat felt wonderful, the tangled mane finally real in his hands.

Their eyes met. The gaze lasted only a second, but was too much for her. She bolted and Kendall's hand slid off her back. He watched her canter across the brush, not galloping yet, but giving him quick, mischievous glances as if wondering if he would follow. A split second later she broke into a full gallop and was gone once more.

Kendall began to jog again. His heart danced wildly with the incredible day.

Back at the pueblo, he washed the sweat off with a basin of water and dressed in clean clothes. He fixed himself a sandwich, then found Mary and Trina at their pottery table near the plaza.

"The summer crowds are getting bigger as we near the ceremonies," Mary told him. "But the pueblo will be closed tomorrow for four days."

"Watch out," Trina teased. "The kachinas might capture you and take you into one of the kivas to scare you."

"Oh, Trina," her mother chided gently.

Corinne stayed at the table while her mother kept Kendall and Trina busy unloading bags of groceries from the pickup truck and carrying them up the ladder.

"We have to fix a lot of food for our guests," Trina said. "Plus, my dad is taking time off from work at the end of the week for the ceremonies."

The Ramirez family would stay on top of Sky City during the days of the ceremonies, but would return to Acomita to sleep, since there wasn't enough room for all of them.

Mary had Kendall and Trina chop vegetables at the table while she put together two pots of soup and kneaded dough for the little round loaves of bread for the oven. There were so many that Kendall began to count them, but his aunt told him to stop. "If we count our food, then we might run out."

"I have more food at our house that I'll bring tomorrow," Mary said while the dough was rising. "I'm going to build a fire in the oven, so why don't you two finish up with the wet clay. I'll need more animals after the dances next week and there won't be time to fire them if we don't get them made now."

Kendall set up a card table while Trina retrieved the bowl of clay from the truck. Trina showed Kendall how to roll the clay into long coils. She rolled out several, then began to build them into a bowl, one on top of the other. Once they were stacked, six coils in all, Trina smoothed the out-side, using a wet finger. When she finished, the tiny bowl was just big enough to fit inside her palm.

"Now I'm going to make a frog to attach to the rim." She took a small lump and began to fashion it into a tiny frog, making miniature legs and a round belly. The whole thing was no more than an inch in size.

Kendall broke off a lump of clay and rolled it between his palms until he had a skinny coil that didn't break. He bent the coil into a zigzag shape for a snake, flattening the top ever so slightly to make it look more real. For the head, Trina showed him how to put in eyes and a slit for a mouth with a forked tongue.

"That's good," Mary commented, coming over to see their work. "Now make me some little ones that I can sell for a few dollars. I also need more frogs and some squirrels and rabbits."

In a couple of hours, Trina had an entire row of miniature animals, including a cat, a bird, and a beaver with a branch of wood in its mouth.

"Those are great," Kendall said.

"Don't touch them until they're dry and we can fire them," Trina warned.

Kendall had made two more snakes, their heads slightly raised. He hoped to paint them with the markings of the rattler, one for his great-grandfather and one for his father as gifts.

Making the snakes was the only way he could think of to participate in the ceremonies ahead. He still wasn't sure if he'd be allowed to witness the dances. Nobody had said anything yet, and he hadn't dared ask. Tomorrow when Armando returned, he would ask him.

Kendall watched Trina turn over her figurines and paint

a picture of a badger on the bottom; in tiny perfect figures, she printed the date.

"What's the badger for?"

"That's our clan symbol."

"Your clan? But I thought you were Snake Clan, like Grandfather."

"No, we're part of my mother's clan, which is Badger."

"How did she get to be Badger?"

"Children take on their mother's clan, and Armando's brother is my great-grandfather. He married a Badger woman, so now all the daughters are Badger. We're part of both our parent's clans, and sometimes husbands who marry will take their wife's clan."

"So my great-grandfather really is the last of the Snake Clan," Kendall said. Both Armando's own daughter and his granddaughter had died. There were no more daughters to carry on the clan.

"My father is Sky Clan. So I'm called Badger Clan, child of Sky," Trina said.

Kendall liked how that sounded.

"My mother said the Snake Clan has been dying for hundreds of years. Many clans are gone now. When she was born there were fourteen, and now there are only twelve. There used to be even more a long time ago, like twenty or something. I don't know what will happen to Armando's Snake Clan house when he dies," Trina added. "I don't know if you could get it, since you're not really Acoma."

Her mother looked up from her cooking.

"Hey, I know what you are!" Trina exclaimed, then laughed. "Snake Clan, child of Anglo."

"It's time to clean up now, Trina," her mother said in a tight voice.

On the second day, pieces of a puzzle whirled in Kendall's head as he helped carry firewood for the baking. Then something clicked so suddenly he almost fell over coming into the house again.

Since he had come here, Kendall understood more clearly the reasons his mother and his great-grandfather had let her marriage cause a permanent rift. Kendall had always known the strong feelings his mother had for her family at Acoma. It had been obvious in everything she said. Armando Abeyta was more than her grandfather, he'd been a *father* to her. He had raised her. She had loved her life here and missed it, especially during the last year she was alive.

His parents had always said the feud was because Dad was Anglo, but it ran much deeper than that. When Mom married outside of Acoma, she disowned herself and pronounced the death of the Snake Clan. She was the last woman to bear Snake Clan offspring, and clans were passed on by the women. When she married Reid Drennan, she gave a death sentence to her clan. She had fallen in love with the wrong man.

Did that make Kendall a mistake? The blood of the Snake Clan, the blood of the runners was strong in him, as strong as if he were full-blooded Acoma. Kendall knew that. And Kendall knew he had to prove that to his great-grandfather and learn about the Snake Runner's ways before it was too late.

He was looking forward to Armando's return. Kendall was surprised at how much he had missed him. He had spent the past night at Acomita with Trina's family, but they were leaving the next day to pick up her father in Albuquerque.

He and Trina finished painting their clay animals and got them ready for firing. At the end of the day, Mary wrapped the last loaves of bread in plastic bags. Trina washed the dishes while Kendall wiped down the clay worktable and put things away. He helped carry stuff to the truck and Mary started the ignition.

"It's time to get home for supper," his aunt said. "I left you a little soup and some vegetables to eat, Kendall. Armando should be here soon. He's probably walking up the path right now."

The last of the tourists boarded the final bus down the hill as Kendall went back to the Abeyta house. That unique time of the evening when Acoma was at last just herself again swept over Kendall. Except for his morning running, this part of the day had to be the best. The sun hadn't yet set, but was disappearing behind the mountains, cliffs burnished gold from centuries of sunsets.

Kendall sat in a folding chair on the roof by himself. He didn't even miss television anymore. It would be odd to go back home after weeks of slow, quiet days.

His great-grandfather should be here soon. Kendall saved the dinner to eat together, although he couldn't help eating one of the little loaves of bread.

Twilight hovered for an hour. He yawned and stood up over and over again to stay awake. It had to be almost nine o' clock. He was so used to getting up at dawn that he was about to fall asleep sitting in the hard chair.

Perhaps Armando had stopped somewhere on his way back. Maybe he was with the medicine man or the cacique or other elders. Occasionally Armando had gone to some of these men's homes for supper and talk while Kendall stayed home and wrote letters to Dad. Once they had cooked for a group of elders themselves, but Kendall didn't understand much of their talk, it being all in Keresan. Even the elder's names were all jumbled together in his brain, and Kendall wasn't sure where any of them lived exactly. Besides, he would never feel comfortable disturbing any of them at their homes.

Kendall put away the chair, climbed down the ladder,

and closed the front door. Hungry, he gulped down some of the stew along with another roll.

He sat on his sleeping bag, getting out the circular object hidden inside his duffel bag and fingering it between his palms. He hadn't looked at it since he'd so impulsively packed it. Kendall held it up to the firelight, and the yellow light shone through the weaving. He still remembered the day his mother had given the dream catcher to him and told him how it caught his dreams, trickling all the good dreams down into the feathers to return another night. Bad dreams were caught in the center and burned off in the first morning light. It had worked all during the years he was young. But the nightmare of the day she died came back again and again, locked in by the dream catcher. Why did it never burn off? Where were the good memories? It seemed as though they had trickled off the feathers, slid around the circle, and disappeared forever.

It was dawn when Kendall woke. He was cold and goose bumps prickled his arms. Kendall shook the hair out of his eyes, feeling dopey and tired. It felt funny to have slept in his clothes.

Then his head cleared and he sat up quickly. He hadn't heard his great-grandfather come in. Kendall rushed to his feet.

The door to Armando's bedroom wasn't completely shut. He listened for the sound of breathing. There was none. Kendall pushed the door open a few inches. It was probably bad manners, but he had to know. Blankets lay neatly tucked in. The bed was still made exactly as the older man had left it the day before.

His great-grandfather had never returned.

16

Kendall was so stunned, he couldn't think. Surely Grandfather hadn't stayed out a second night. It didn't seem like
he would do that.

What should he do? Think, Kendall ordered himself. First
he'd call Mary at Acomita, ten miles away. But there weren't
phones on top of Sky City and the visitor's center was
locked until eight, so that wasn't an option.

Armando had said he would be back for dinner. He
wouldn't say that and then not come back. Something had
to have happened to him. Perhaps he had become ill or
gotten hurt. No, that couldn't have happened to a man who
had lived here his entire life and run miles every day. But
Kendall also knew his great-grandfather should have been
home nearly twelve hours ago. And he was old, even if he
was still healthy and strong.

He should never have gone to sleep last night. Too many
hours had passed already.

Kendall didn't want to wait until eight o'clock. It was
barely five now. If he was going to run ten miles, he'd rather
run into the desert to find his great-grandfather than waste

energy and time running those miles to Acomita in the opposite direction.

Then Kendall remembered that going to Acomita wasn't an option either. Mary and her daughters were leaving early today to drive to Albuquerque to shop and to pick Mr. Ramirez up from the airport.

As his mind ticked off the possibilities, Kendall fumbled through his clothes to dress for running. After a moment he made himself stop. He couldn't just rush out without any planning and without being prepared.

Kendall slowed down long enough to perform the running rituals. He needed all the help he could get from the gods. If he wasn't in the right frame of mind, he wouldn't be able to find his great-grandfather.

Step by step Kendall went through the preparations. He tied the bundles to his waist and filled his water pouch. He tucked a loaf of bread in also in case his great-grandfather needed food. Kendall decided he would not eat. Armando had told him of the times men fasted for days, not eating until they had received their visions and dreams. If fasting brought such gifts from the gods, then he would fast to bring him success at finding his great-grandfather. Last of all, he wrapped the bandanna around his forehead, pulling back the hair that now almost touched his neck.

He hurried to the door, anxious to be on his way. Then he suddenly stopped and returned to a kitchen drawer to find a piece of paper and pencil. Hurriedly he scribbled a note to Mary and left it on the table.

Closing the front door, Kendall knew he had done everything he could to be ready for what lay ahead. The village silence seemed filled with spirits who waited to see what he would or could do.

Not a breeze touched Sky City. It was the quietest dawn. Kendall felt the magic cord stretching from his heart all the way to Katzima, and beyond. Columns of dark clouds filled the sky above, waiting for the dances and rituals before they let loose their rain.

Somewhere out in the desert, his great-grandfather was waiting for Kendall to run to him.

He knew he was prepared to run far and long. The miles to Enchanted Mesa were easy now. If he had to go several more miles to find his great-grandfather, no problem. He'd still be back by late afternoon.

Kendall climbed down the cliffs of Acoma, then closed his eyes while he took several deep breaths. Reaching out toward the power that spanned the valley, he began to run.

When he reached Enchanted Mesa, Kendall started feeling a little foolish. Had he gone off too fast? Had his great-grandfather decided to stay a second night to pray and fast? This could end up being a wild-goose chase and he'd miss connecting with Armando out on the desert completely. Kendall didn't really know which direction the old man had gone.

He circled Katzima, willing the mesa to speak to him and tell him what to do. It was time. Past time.

"Help me!" he cried. "Please."

As always, the mesa said nothing. But the longer Kendall stood in the shadow of the golden walls, the more he knew his great-grandfather needed him. He felt the swelling spirit of the magic grow and fill his legs and soul. Roads ended out here. It was land only for a runner.

Where was Rasmiyah? Kendall had hoped to see her, to run beside her and touch her warm neck again. He had a silly hope that she would know where Armando was and take him there, but there wasn't any sign of the herd of horses today. Kendall sipped his water, then tied the pouch up again.

South. Suddenly Kendall remembered. That was the direction his great-grandfather had said he ran in his youth. Kendall would head south straight for the ridge of mesas in the distance, keeping Enchanted Mesa directly behind him for a landmark.

He rubbed his legs down, ignored his hungry stomach, and set off.

The terrain grew rougher the farther he ran. Small ravines slowed him down. He kept an eye out for gopher holes and the barbed cacti.

He hadn't gone more than two or three miles past Enchanted Mesa when Kendall halted in the valley floor. It couldn't be. He was seeing double. Had he just run in a big circle or were his eyes playing tricks?

Just a mile up ahead was Enchanted Mesa. Kendall whipped around to look behind him. There was Enchanted Mesa to the north, distant but still huge under the sweltering sun. He faced south again. Enchanted Mesa stood in front of him. He twisted in a circle, confused. But this time he realized that the mesa farther south looked like a miniature version of Enchanted Mesa.

Kendall sped up, anxious to reach it. He was thankful for the cloud cover as the morning turned warmer. Sweat dripped down his face despite the flat grayness of the sky.

The closer he got to the second mesa, the harder the magic throbbed in his legs and chest. It was almost like a force field that pulled him to this miniature Enchanted Mesa. His whole body tingled and surged with the swells of magic.

He stopped in the shade of the walls. Kendall trembled with the power radiating from this place. He felt as if he had stepped on sacred ground. This replica of Enchanted Mesa was exquisite, about two hundred feet high and half a mile around the base. The top was a little more rocky and uneven than Katzima, but the walls were just as steep, wrapped with smudges of rose-colored pink like a ribbon.

Kendall could hardly catch his breath. He couldn't stay here—the magic was more than he could bear. He had to push on, but he was glad to have the second mesa as another landmark so that he didn't get lost.

After another couple of hours, he stopped for more water. His pace was about half his usual speed and he had no idea how far he'd run.

Fatigue was hitting hard. His vision was blurring and his limbs were beginning to go numb. Still there was no sign of Armando. Was he close to the southern shrine at all? The ring of mountains at the edge of the valley had been growing larger and closer with every mile. Another three miles and he'd be there. He hoped. Clouds stained the sky purple.

Kendall sensed that it was high noon now, although it was hard to judge without seeing the sun clearly. He knew there was no chance of rain yet. Not for a few more days. Not until after the dances.

He pushed on, his legs growing heavier and more rubbery with each step. Kendall tried not to think about the distance back to Sky City. And he didn't drink any more water. It had to last a lot of return miles.

When he came over another rise in the terrain, Kendall let out a yell and almost ran right into the rattlesnake lying coiled on the rocky earth. Kendall heard the rattle before he even saw the tail shake, sounding like pebbles in a tin can.

He froze instantly, but couldn't stop from coughing, throat burning so much he couldn't even swallow. The snake's head shot up, tongue flicking three feet from Kendall's moccasins, way too close. He wondered how fast a snake could move. Fast, he thought.

How long could he pretend to be a rock?

Not very long. He desperately wanted to cough. Tears ran down both cheeks with the effort to hold it back.

He knew he should feel more afraid, but today was different. Today he *was* Acoma. He had run this desert valley like no one had done for years. And he belonged to the Snake Clan, no matter what Trina said.

Kendall closed his eyes, remembering what his great-grandfather had told him about the reasons of reverence for the mystical reptile. "Snakes can move without aid of feet or limbs." Armando's voice echoed in his head. "They have the power of hypnosis over any man or beast. A snake achieves immortality through its ability to shed its skin and live again. And the bite of the snake is deadly."

He had to get away from this snake. The bundles dragged at Kendall's waist and the heavy stone pulled at his neck. Fresh sweat dripped into his eyes as the rattlesnake slithered closer. Kendall wondered if he should make a dash for it. Could he outrun the creature before it sprang forward and sank its fangs into his skin?

The sand whispered as the reptile skimmed closer, zig-zagging like a lightning bolt; then it began to coil again, wrapping itself into a ball, head and neck swaying upward. Its slitted black eyes stared into Kendall's face.

He had no choice but to stare back. Kendall imagined himself sweeping that rattler clean off the ground with one hand. Of course he wasn't fool enough to try. But he had the fastest hundred-yard dash in the history of his elementary school.

And he had the shimmering magic cord to help him. Kendall slowly breathed in, gathering his wits and last bit of strength. The rattler's tail lifted, and shook. There was a flash of sharp, curved fangs.

The rock Kendall had become melted, and with a blood-curdling cry from his dry throat, he bolted the moment the snake leaped for him.

Kendall felt the reptile's skin brush against his leg, but the serpent's teeth missed his flesh. Within a second, Kendall was yards away and running faster than he had all day. He ran and ran, not daring to glance backward. Just concentrated on the harsh terrain below his feet so as not to fall. He ran another quarter mile, then looked up to see where he was.

The foot of the mountains loomed ahead.

17

Kendall scanned the foothills and surrounding desert floor. There wasn't a single sign of his great-grandfather. He fell down onto the dirt, legs trembling uncontrollably. He had no idea how far into the afternoon it was.

Reaching for his water pouch, he drank one sip and held the cool bag to his face. He was in the middle of nowhere. It was an odd feeling. But the valley felt like a comforting blanket enclosing him. He had to trust in that.

Kendall finally got up and began to scramble through the foothills searching for any sign of his great-grandfather. His biggest worry was that the elderly man was somewhere out in the desert and Kendall had overlooked him. But that seemed impossible. On the flat desert valley floor one could see for miles. Surely he wouldn't have missed him.

Climbing higher on the mountain, Kendall cut his hands on the rocks. Blood oozed and he smeared the sticky red stuff against his thigh. When he heard low rumbling in the distance, Kendall glanced up. It seemed to be getting darker, but maybe that was just the black storm clouds. Kendall felt his pulse thudding in his throat.

Pushing back the bandanna, Kendall tried not to panic. He shaded his eyes, searching the mountain with its rocks and boulders again and again. His eyes finally focused on a bundle of sticks that looked out of place among the sand and brush. Kendall's heart jumped.

He struggled over the remaining boulders and the ground sloped downward into a small hidden indentation in the earth. It was the shrine. He knew it instantly.

Flat rocks had been stacked like bricks at the opening. Pieces of wood in various shapes and sizes had been laid in rows across the top of the rocks. Kachinas, prayer sticks, and feathers had been placed all around the shrine, guarding the entrance. As Kendall looked closer, he realized the stacks of firewood were actually carvings. The sticks were decorated with drawings of faces, bears, birds, lightning, and clan symbols.

Near the bottom of the entrance, a handmade dream catcher just like the one his mother had given him dangled from a piece of leather.

Kendall didn't touch anything. He knelt and said his own silent prayer that he would be able to find his great-grandfather before dark descended. The moment he rose from his knees, Kendall knew Armando had made it here. He recognized a freshly painted prayer stick laid on top of the piles of offerings. It was the one his great-grandfather had taken with him.

Okay, so where was Armando now? Kendall scanned the mountain he'd just climbed. Which way had his great-grandfather gone when he left the shrine? There didn't seem to be a clue.

Kendall had no choice but to descend. His eyes darted about as he made his way back down through the rocks and boulders and dips in the earth.

Had he been an idiot to run all the way out here on

a wild-goose chase? His heart told him the magic had led the way.

Kendall had almost reached the bottom of the mountain when he heard a clatter of rocks. His stomach jumped. Another snake? Reptiles often set up residence under rocks, and Kendall had been careful to watch out for them on the ridge.

Heart pumping, he crept over to the sound. He couldn't see anything. The landscape blended together and Kendall wiped his eyes, unable to stop them from watering. Panic and fear grew stronger with every passing moment.

"Kendall," the wind whispered.

He jumped, thinking the rocks had come alive. Or maybe it was the gods talking. Nothing else was around. At least nothing that was visible. He must be hallucinating now, his mind or ears playing tricks on him.

Kendall stepped between two boulders, expecting a winged serpent to capture him and carry him up to the clouds. There was no mythical creature, just empty desert. Man, was he spooked!

He looked down to watch his next step and saw an arm lying stretched out behind the rocks. At first Kendall jumped, he was so startled, but then relief flooded his body, making him weak. He tried to call out, but found his voice was gone.

Clambering back down the boulders, Kendall dropped to his knees in front of Armando. He reached out to touch the elderly man and make sure he was real. He couldn't believe that he'd actually found him. But his great-grandfather wasn't a mirage. He was real. Kendall stroked his arm and his face, then leaned close to brush the elderly man's cheek with his own.

"Grandfather," he whispered. "What happened?"

"Is it you, Grandson?" the elderly man croaked behind half-opened eyes. "Or are you a spirit sent from the gods?"

Armando's face was gray. His bandanna was torn and dried blood was caked across his forehead. The old man lay wedged next to the boulder, and the objects from his bag had spilled out all over the area.

"I've broken my leg. And cracked a couple of ribs."

"I think you might have a concussion, too," Kendall told him.

Armando shifted his shoulders in agreement. He wheezed painfully and could hardly speak. "Sometimes I wake and sometimes I sleep."

Kendall could tell every breath was torture. "You're having a hard time breathing. It's more than just cracked ribs."

The elderly man closed his eyes. So much time passed that Kendall wondered if Armando had fallen asleep or passed out. But the heavy lids fluttered again.

"My lungs," he began to mutter.

"What do you want me to do?" Kendall asked. "I'll stay with you."

Armando clutched his hand. "You must run and get a truck for me."

"I don't want to leave you alone," Kendall said, but he knew he had to leave his great-grandfather to get help. There was no way the older man could get back on his own. And if he didn't go for help, his great-grandfather might die.

"I will pray for you as you run, boy," Armando said.

Kendall rocked back on his heels, contemplating what he was about to do. There was no other choice.

He had to run back to Acoma right now. The thought was utterly daunting. He was so tired he could have fallen asleep on the hard rocks that very instant.

Darkness wasn't far away. He'd be running without light. What if he got lost? He couldn't get lost. In order to beat the darkness, he had to run faster than the sun set until he reached Katzima, or at least its miniature shadow, so that he had a landmark before the night turned black.

Kendall rubbed his arms and legs briskly. He wanted herbs, prayers, food, and sleep. He blinked back the painful burning behind his eyes caused by fatigue. He had the gods, the prayers of his great-grandfather, and the magic to help him. It was enough. It had to be.

He dug out the bread, glad now he hadn't eaten it. "Here, have some of this." Breaking the bread into bite-sized pieces, he placed one in Armando's mouth; then Kendall helped him drink from the water pouch.

The elderly man sighed. "That's good. I'm on my sacred mountain. I'm not worried about the future. Only let me hold my prayer stick."

Kendall quickly gathered the items that had scattered and pressed them into the old man's cold, waxy hands.

"Now you must go," Armando commanded. "Don't run too fast and fall yourself. Be careful."

"I will." Kendall stood to leave, torn at having to go but anxious to get help.

Then his great-grandfather beckoned him back. "There are things I must say to you before you leave," he murmured between his cracked lips.

"I need to hurry, Grandfather. The sun is moving down the sky."

"The Snake Clan will end with you."

Kendall shook his head, biting back the emotion that tugged at his face, but he knew it was true.

"They will train you in the kiva. You are getting too old to put it off much longer. Your manhood is soon."

"Oh, Grandfather," Kendall said, overwhelmed. He wiped his watery nose with his arm.

"It is a decision I have already discussed with the elders, and they have approved. I came here for many reasons.

"This old snake . . ." Armando paused for breath and his face wore the pain he suffered. "I will soon shed my skin and go on with the spirits."

"Don't talk anymore," Kendall pleaded. "I'll be back as fast as I can with a car to get you out of here."

Armando lifted his hand as Kendall took deep, long breaths to prepare for his run. His stomach had grown tight without any food all day, but he wasn't hungry anymore. He had never fasted before, but it seemed to be giving him renewed strength, a kind he had never felt before. Strength from a well deep within his soul. A well not known to him before now, but one only waiting to be discovered.

He reached out to the magic waves stretching across the valley. That magical trembling cord would take him home.

As he scrambled down the slope, his legs protested. They felt like two dead tree stumps. How could he possibly make it? Kendall clung to the quivering magic strands and hung on, trying to ignore his knotted muscles, his sore throat, the numbness in his limbs.

He began running and couldn't seem to get his legs to move any faster than a jog. He had to keep stopping to rest. Again and again he pushed his legs forward, only to half run a few yards and then stop again.

In the middle of the desert, he felt completely isolated except for the magic, the only thing that kept him from collapsing right onto the stony ground.

His entire body was consumed with mindless misery. Every step took great effort. It wasn't even running anymore.

Tears rolled down his face and neck, making streaks in the dirt. Kendall tried not to blubber like a baby, but tears kept flowing.

"Rasmiyah," Kendall whispered through bleeding lips. "Where are you? I need you." If only Rasmiyah would allow him to ride her the rest of the way to Sky City. It was a futile hope. She barely let him close enough to touch her. She would never let him ride her. This was his test as an Acoma runner.

The sun finally disappeared behind the far ridges. Dusk deepened, and Kendall thought about the hours until sunrise. By then he might be crippled.

Kendall pushed on, even though it was sheer torture. His arms dragged at his sides, and his feet were blistered under the moccasins.

He fell. Rocks gouged his knees. Crouched on all fours like a dog, Kendall strained to see ahead into the darkness. He fought himself to get up again.

Lifting his head, Kendall saw two pinpoints of light. Could that actually be Sky City? But if that was the village up ahead, where had Enchanted Mesa disappeared to? How could he have passed the citadel and not known it?

He must be hallucinating. The flickering rays seemed to jump around in the dark. Perhaps they were the eyes of a mountain lion closing in on him. Kendall felt a burst of rage. He hadn't come all this way just to get eaten by a wild animal in the dark. The lights began to grow; a little bigger, brighter, beckoning him. This wasn't any wild animal. Those shafts of white would take him home to Sky City, home to get help. He had to be close, and the glow was coming from the right direction.

Groaning with pain, he staggered to his feet. He took two steps and swayed like a drunk man. Strange noises rumbled to his left and Kendall felt the vibrations of a vehicle approaching. The two beams swelled into headlights and Kendall could see his own silhouette shadowed against the desert. A door opened and slammed, the engine idling.

Trina's loud voice came out of the darkness. "Kendall, is that you?"

He couldn't speak. His voice was gone.

"We got your note and we've been driving for two hours looking for you."

Then Kendall felt Mary's warm arms wrap around his shoulders. "Where's your grandfather?" she asked.

"At the southern shrine," Kendall croaked, and dropped again to the earth. He couldn't stop the tears of relief flowing down his face. "I can take you."

Without another word, Trina and Mary helped him to his feet and Kendall climbed into the cab of the truck, every muscle in his body protesting. When Trina had slammed the door shut, she asked, "Can the truck make it even farther into the desert?"

"We will make it," Mary replied without hesitation. She put the truck into four-wheel drive and flicked on her brights.

Kendall slumped back against the seat, giving directions now and then as he recognized the terrain he had just crossed.

"Let me know if I turn off in the wrong direction," Mary instructed Kendall. "I've never actually been to the shrine itself. Only the men are allowed to go. I don't know how you found it." She glanced over at him, questions in her eyes.

Kendall wasn't quite sure either. He couldn't explain the magic that had taken him there. He hardly dared believe it himself.

The truck jostled over dips, sudden holes, and twists. Once Trina elbowed him when the truck went careening to the side over a particularly deep rut.

"Sorry," she said softly, and there was a different sound to her voice.

Kendall gave a grunt. "That's okay. I've got more bruises than I can count."

"Kendall," she said, leaning closer to be heard over the engine, but speaking so that her mother could not overhear, "you really ran over all this desert? All these miles?"

"Limped mostly. Took too long." It was hard to speak. Words stuck in Kendall's swollen throat.

"I don't think I could have done that. Ever. I don't think many people could have," she said, and quickly sat up again as if she hadn't spoken at all.

Kendall leaned forward as the sacred hills came into view in the headlights. "Stop there. Grandfather is behind the boulders."

Mary pulled the truck up as far as she could, set the gear in park, but left the engine and lights running.

Kendall pushed open the door and stumbled over the rocks to where he had left the elderly man. "Grandfather," he called, wishing he had a flashlight, it was so dark behind the rocks. He dropped to his knees, not even feeling the scrapes and bruises any longer.

"Mary's here with the truck to get you to the hospital."

His great-grandfather gripped his upper arm. "You are real, Grandson. I'm not dreaming, then."

"No, you're not dreaming," Kendall assured him. "You're going to be all right."

Mary appeared behind him in the dark. "I've got blankets in the back of the truck to make a bed."

"Get the medicine man," Armando said.

Kendall could tell that every word he spoke was excruciating. He worried about the internal damage his great-grandfather had done falling on the boulders.

Kendall and Mary were able to raise Armando to his feet. It was difficult to keep his leg intact and not crush his ribs any more as they helped him into the bed of the Chevy, where Trina had laid down the wool blankets and pillows.

"He's going to hurt as we go back," Kendall said. "I'm going to stay with him."

Mary nodded. "My husband is gathering the elders. Don't worry, Kendall. I'm sure Armando will be fine."

Kendall laid a blanket over Armando and helped him drink the last of the water from the leather pouch. He checked to make sure he had collected the belongings from his great-grandfather's sacred bundle, then fastened it to Armando's leather trousers. Kendall eased down beside the old man, and as he did, every bone and muscle in his own body collapsed into the blankets.

The truck swung from side to side as Mary turned, popped the clutch into gear, and headed back.

His great-grandfather's breathing was shallow. Kendall put up a hand to feel the man's forehead and neck. He was burning with fever.

"Lie down," Armando told him, reaching for Kendall's hand. "Together we will sleep for a little while."

Kendall listened to the truck grinding over rocks and jagged ruts. It was a good thing there hadn't been rain yet. Mud would have made it impassable.

After a few miles, Kendall thought for sure his great-grandfather had gone unconscious, but then he heard words coming through the darkness over the truck engine. "Come here, Kendall."

Rolling over slowly, Kendall saw brilliant sharp stars under a black velvet sky arching over the Acoma desert. He moved closer and Armando clenched his hand with surprising strength.

"Tonight I leave this world for Si-pa-pu and return to the world of the spirits."

"No," Kendall protested, unable to think of his great-grandfather dying. "It's not time for you to go there. Not yet."

"I know you are weary, Grandson, but sacred visions come to those who sacrifice."

Kendall felt his mouth trembling. "I'm still waiting for my visions, Grandfather."

"The miles you ran today could not have been done by an ordinary boy or an ordinary runner. The gods will not forget what you have done for me. I will not become a skeleton alone in the desert. I can die in my home on the sacred cliffs of Acoma and be laid beside my family."

Armando's voice faltered, but the elderly man pushed past the pain. "This day you will remember until you are an old man yourself."

Kendall tried to speak and the emotions he felt would not shape into words. He could only nod, but he knew that he would never forget this day.

His great-grandfather lifted Kendall's hand to his face and pressed it against his wrinkled skin. "Today, my son, you are an Acoma runner. I shed my skin on you. You are my young skin again, the last of the Snakes, until the day you die."

18

The medicine man and the elders were gathering at the pueblo when Mary maneuvered the vehicle down the narrow streets and parked in front of the ladder to the Abeyta home. Silence enfolded the world when the truck's engine was shut off. Armando was unconscious, and Kendall could hardly drag himself up the rungs of the ladder into the house.

Without speaking, the group of men carried his great-grandfather inside and laid him on the bed in the back room.

Kendall fell asleep to the sounds of singing and the chants of the medicine man healing his great-grandfather. When he woke, Mary was building a fire on the hearth. The medicine man sat cross-legged on the floor beside the blankets.

Embarrassed, Kendall sat up and quickly pulled on his shirt. He groaned out loud when his stiff limbs protested every movement. He knew he could stay in bed for days. As soon as his great-grandfather was well, he would do just that. But right now he wanted to see him.

The medicine man watched Kendall dress without speaking. When Mary left the room to go into the kitchen, the man held up a hand to stop Kendall at the door to the bedroom. "Come here, young man."

Kendall sat down on the floor in front of him. The carving of a bear dangled from a leather strap around the older man's neck.

The medicine man sat with his eyes closed for a moment, then opened them to look at Kendall. "Your great-grandfather would not leave Acoma for surgery. His warrior wounds could not be healed with herbs and rituals. Too much inside his body was hurt."

Kendall felt a catch in his throat. His mind did not want to comprehend the man's words. He tried to speak, but no words passed his swollen mouth. The medicine man just watched him, compassion in his eyes. Kendall stumbled to his feet, flinging himself to the bedroom door.

Armando lay still under the blankets, the gash on his forehead wiped clean, his long white hair freshly brushed and spread across the pillow.

Kendall reached out a hand to touch his great-grandfather's fingers resting on the colorful blanket. The skin felt smooth and cold. His great-grandfather's spirit was already gone.

Armando was a man who had run his whole life for his dreams, his gods, his people. This wasn't how he was supposed to die.

The medicine man came up behind him. "His last words were for you," came the quiet, kind voice. "He asked me to take his place as your spiritual adviser. I will train you in the kiva and be your teacher. If all goes well, perhaps next summer you can be initiated into the warrior society as your great-grandfather was."

Kendall held back the flood that threatened to pour down

his face. He couldn't cry in front of this man. Not yet, not here.

"You are to be registered as Acoma if you so choose. Your name will be declared as the last surviving member of the Snake Clan."

"He wasn't supposed to die," Kendall stammered. "He was going to tell me about the Snake Dance and what the ancient runners did hundreds of years ago."

"All tribes suffer the loss of clan traditions. It is the way with this new world we must live in. The last member of the Snake Clan who knew the old ways has died this day."

For a strange, bitter moment, Kendall glimpsed what Armando had felt. Acoma had survived centuries of drought, starvation, conquerors, and death. It had survived, but not intact. People left and clans died.

What could a half-Anglo boy do to prevent that? Kendall knew nothing about the true essence of the Acomas' belief and religion, very little about their ceremonies and rituals. His chance couldn't be gone already. It couldn't!

Kendall felt the elder's presence beside him. "Can you tell me of these old ways?" he asked.

The medicine man shook his head. "I am not of the Snake Clan. The Snake Dance was lost to us hundreds of years ago. Your great-grandfather was the last to carry the knowledge."

"So it's gone forever?" It didn't seem possible. It wasn't fair. He was here to run, to learn about the snake clan and carry it on, and it was already too late. Only a few weeks had passed this summer, and the chance was gone forever.

Turning his face away, Kendall wiped at his eyes like a kid, trying to hide it from the elder. Silent, the medicine man left the bedroom to give him privacy.

Stepping closer, Kendall crawled up on the bed next to his great-grandfather lying so peaceful and handsome on the blankets. Years had faded from the old man's face. Kendall wanted to wake up the warrior, shake the runner from the past alive again.

Why had Kendall been given the magic, the power to run, if it was all lost?

The medicine man returned and beckoned him. "You must not stay with the body. His spirit will linger for four days here in this home, and it might be powerful enough to take you with him. We must do the death rituals and cleansing."

Another man came into the room and Kendall backed out of their way. He fell onto his sleeping bag by the fire pit, his whole body hurting so badly he thought he might be ill.

For the next few hours, Kendall listened to the sound of drums and chants and then to the final prayers as the medicine man bid farewell to Armando's spirit. Kendall woke up again in the afternoon as Trina and her family came to sprinkle cornmeal and leave gifts of food, as did many other villagers and Armando's friends.

Visitors came and went until dusk. Kendall watched as the elders wrapped his great-grandfather's body in a scarlet blanket. Then six men lifted him out the door and down the ladder to the church cemetery for burial. A prayer stick was left where Armando had lain.

"In four days, we will gather the feathered stick and take it to the gate of Si-pa-pu to the west," the medicine man told Kendall.

It was another wound. Not only was his chance to know about the runners and the Snake Dance taken away from him, but his last chance to ask his great-grandfather to give a message to his mother at Si-pa-pu was gone. It was too late for everything.

Mary, her husband, her daughters, and a procession of

villagers followed Kendall and the bearers of Armando's body down the narrow streets.

A grave had already been dug next to that of Armando's wife, Lydia Abeyta, in the cemetery lot in front of the church steps. The churchyard was enclosed by an adobe wall that paralleled the border of the southern cliffs.

A distant drumming penetrated the very ground Kendall stood on, a beat that seemed to come up from the earth itself. He felt dizzy with exhaustion and lack of food. But he could only stand there, unable to think about a future as a runner without Armando to help him.

When Armando had been laid inside the earth, Mary stepped forward with a clay pitcher. She broke the jar and water spilled in trickles over the casket.

"His last drink," someone murmured behind Kendall.

Mary came toward Kendall, cornmeal in her hands. She placed some in each of his palms and showed him how to throw it across the open grave. Trina and Corinne imitated their mother in this final gesture of farewell. Then the pallbearers picked up their shovels and began to throw the mound of dirt back into the hole.

The church bells suddenly pealed, four slow strokes. Then the ringing stopped. The villagers returned to their homes and Kendall watched the diggers finish filling the grave.

Mary touched Kendall's arm. "Come home with us to Acomita. The dances begin tomorrow. The ceremonies were delayed for Armando's burial, but they cannot wait any longer. There are signs of the kachinas close at hand."

Kendall shook his head, "No, I want to stay here at Old Acoma."

Mary pressed further. "After four days we must cleanse and purify ourselves. I will help you."

"I can't go with you." He broke away from her and ran

back home, clumsily, painfully climbing the ladder rungs. As Kendall shut the door, he could hear the drums pounding inside the kivas.

The house was deathly quiet. Kendall ached with grief. He knew he had to call Dad, but he hadn't had a chance. Less than twenty-four hours had passed since bringing Armando in the truck from the desert.

He stayed in bed through that night and the next day. There was plenty of food, but Kendall couldn't eat it. As he drifted in and out of sleep, he listened to the faraway drumming and singing.

Dancers returned to the kivas for more rites. Kendall watched the shadows in the room change with the sun's own ritual pattern. The next morning, as he was turning groggily in his sleeping bag, Trina burst through the door. "Kendall!" she called, banging the screen door. She paused in the doorway to the main room, and Kendall could see her figure outlined against the morning light. She wore her manta dress and jewelry, along with the white moccasin leggings that the women used for ceremonies.

Kendall tried to sit up and was suddenly aware that he didn't have a shirt on. He hadn't even brushed his teeth in two days.

Trina moved through the door and knelt on the floor beside him, the jewelry and beads on her wrists tinkling. "How do you feel?"

"Tired," Kendall said, falling back on his pillow.

"I've come to get you for the kachina dances."

"Why? I thought I wasn't invited."

Trina lowered her head and folded her hands in her lap. "My mother told me that Armando had spoken with the elders before he died and told them you were to come and witness the sacred ceremonies for rain." She lifted her eyes to look at him. "That you had to see for yourself the gods bringing the rain."

"Did Mary send you to tell me this?"

"No. I asked my mother if I could come. I wanted to bring you myself."

Kendall rolled over and grabbed a shirt, throwing it over his head. He groaned with the ache of stiff, knotted muscles.

"Are you okay?" Trina asked again. She sounded as though she really wanted to know.

Kendall nodded and gazed at her. Her ceremonial clothing was exquisite. Her eyes were happy and her black hair shone like water. "You look really nice," he said.

"Thank you," she said primly. "Now come on! You don't want to miss any more."

Kendall looked into her face and knew she meant it. "Thanks, cousin," he said.

Then Trina stood up and held out her hands. "Get up, lazybones! I don't want to miss the ceremonies or my mother's food afterwards."

Kendall allowed her to help him up, and when he was on his feet, they grinned at each other. She waited outside while he finished dressing and washing.

Black thunderheads obscured the sky all day long. While thunder rumbled and lightning flashed, the men, hidden beneath kachina masks and wearing special dress, danced around the village and central square. For the four days of rain ceremonies they had become as the gods themselves.

The elders and war chiefs sat on a platform at one end of the square. People crowded all around, some standing on the roofs overlooking the plaza for a better view. Kendall felt spatters of rain, but it disappeared as quickly as it fell.

At the end of the dances, the kachinas threw presents to the crowd. Small girls received handmade dolls. Great baskets of fruit and candy were brought out and tossed to the eager spectators. Children ran to pick up the candy when it fell to the ground. When the masked kachinas left to retrieve their prayer sticks, the people began to disperse quietly back to their homes, hoping the rain would soon come.

Kendall took a basket of food and fruit back to Armando's home and left it on the kitchen table. He couldn't stand up any longer and told Mary and Trina that he had to lie down again.

Mary hugged him as she left. "Get your rest and you'll feel better in a few days. Your father will be arriving soon, too, although Acoma is closed these four days. He will have to wait outside the gates until it's over."

Back on his sleeping bag, Kendall squeezed his eyes shut to keep the tears from running down his face. Even though he was glad to have been allowed to attend the ceremonies, he still felt alone and empty. He wanted to see his dad. But mostly he wanted Armando back. The image of the great runner lying peacefully on his bed in death wouldn't leave his mind. He wanted to go back in time and do everything all over again—leave sooner to find Armando, tell him goodbye properly, beg him to share the secrets of the Snake Runners.

And he hadn't found his mother here. Why hadn't Enchanted Mesa spoken to him? What more was he supposed to do?

Kendall wrapped his arms around the pillow and buried his face in it to keep from sobbing out loud. Everything had happened so fast. Death was like that. Even when you were prepared for it, like with his mom, it had a way of taking you in its grip unexpectedly. They knew for months she was going to die. Kendall thought he was ready, but when it happened, he found out that he really hadn't known what the pain would be like.

Staring upward at the beams in the mud ceiling, Kendall

let the tears spill until there weren't any left. He didn't move the rest of the day. At dusk a light tap sounded on the door, startling him.

He waited for Mary or Trina to appear, but they didn't. The knocking came a second time, more loudly. Kendall got up off the floor and opened the door. Three figures stood in the dark shadows: a tribal police officer, one of the elders, and his father.

"Kendall, are you okay?" Dad exclaimed, grabbing Kendall in a bear hug. "Oh, son, I'm so sorry."

The officer and the elder nudged Kendall's father into the house and closed the door on the streets behind them. The two men stood inside by the door as Dad looked Kendall over and hugged him again.

"How did you get up to Sky City?" Kendall asked.

"Your father's been at the highway since this morning," the policeman said. "The entire reservation is closed and the gates are guarded. He had to wait until the ceremonies were finished for the day."

"Because of Armando's death and with you here alone, they gave me special permission to come up and get you." He held Kendall out to look at him, a mixture of joy and sorrow in his eyes.

The officer stepped outside the front door to wait and the elder sat at the kitchen table while Kendall led Dad into the main room.

Sinking into a chair, his father breathed out a sigh. "I didn't think they'd let me in. Mary reached me in the middle of the night through the truck dispatcher, but I was already on my way."

"You missed the funeral."

"I really wish I could have been here for that. What an awful summer you've had, buddy."

Kendall jumped up from the floor, wincing with pain. "It

hasn't been awful at all, Dad. It's the best summer I could have had after Mom—"

His father's forehead wrinkled. "I guess it was good for you to meet your great-grandfather even though he was old and sick."

"He wasn't sick, Dad. He was . . ." Kendall stopped and shook his head, frustrated. "I can't explain it right now."

"It's time to take you home, son. I really want you to come. Brett's with the truck out on I-40 waiting for us."

"I'll go home with you," Kendall said, but inside he felt frantic. How could he leave? It wasn't finished. Nothing was finished. And all of a sudden he knew what lay ahead of him. The last step on his running journey.

There were questions all over his father's face.

"Dad, there's still something I have to do first."

The magical vibrations rushed through his arms and legs. They'd never really stopped, not even since the funeral. Kendall had spent the hours ignoring the feelings pulling at him. Now the powers tugged him across the room and into the leather apron. Kendall tied on the sacred bundle, flung the stone necklace over his long hair, and began to rub his legs with the herbs and hemlock.

His father stared at him, mouth open, watching each ritual, but he didn't utter a single word.

Kendall stepped across the room and retrieved the water pouch from its place next to the pictures of the Acoma runners. He studied each man's lean body, then gazed into his great-grandfather's youthful face as he stood on the mesa floor decades ago, lightning streaks racing down his thighs.

Armando had joined the runners from the past in the next world. And now Kendall had become one of them. He removed the old picture from its frame and tucked it into his sacred bundle. His great-grandfather would run next to his heart from now on.

He went past the kitchen table to the front door. Kendall knew that tonight the gods were close and he would not look out of place.

The elder stood up from the table, a small man wearing the men's traditional bandanna. "Run tonight for your grandfather. For the Snake Clan."

Behind Kendall, Dad made a funny, choking sound as if to speak.

He looked back to see his father poised on the adobe floor. Kendall opened the water pouch and took a drink, the familiar taste mingled with buckskin running down his throat.

"I'll meet you at the truck, okay?" he told his dad.

His father's jaw moved. "Sure. I'll grab your duffel. Are you okay, buddy?"

Sealing the water pouch, Kendall tied it to his waist again. He nodded and smiled at his father. Then he closed the door and descended the ladder into the pale moonlit streets.

Kendall knew he was foolish. How could he run when he could barely walk? But the cords wrapped around his ankles and drew him urgently across the village. Clouds swallowed up the moon. Tonight anything could happen. The gods roamed Acoma Valley. The people were pure and waiting for rain.

Thunder and lightning cracked nearby. The descent down the mesa was scary in the dark, hanging on to the edge of the cliff with trembling arms. The hairs on the back of Kendall's neck stood on end as he reached the bottom and stared ahead into a night empty of stars or moon. The unknown blackness didn't scare him any longer. Two nights ago he had run in the dark—in the face of danger, exhaustion, rattlesnakes, and death.

Below the clouds, below the moon, Enchanted Mesa waited for him.

Kendall began to run, slipping his hands along the magic cords, trembling at the strength the enchantment gave him, awed at the power. He could run all night again if he had to. He would if it would bring back his mother. If it would bring back his great-grandfather.

The three miles had never seemed so long before. With little food and still sick from so many miles two days before, Kendall pushed forward as best as he could, the magic squeezing him until he thought he would drop.

But Kendall felt no pain except that which was in his heart. Barefoot, he raced into the darkness, the cold wind whipping his hair, thunder so loud he couldn't even hear himself breathing.

The boulders stopped him from running straight into the mesa. Panting, he clambered over the huge piles of rocks. A moment after he touched the walls of Katzima, the boiling clouds opened to release their burden. But it was more than rain, more than a downpour.

Staring at the top of the flat mountain, Kendall watched the torrent of rain cascade over the sharp edges of Enchanted Mesa. It rushed like a river down the labyrinth of crevices. Hugging the rock, Kendall raised his face, and it was like standing in a warm shower.

He pushed himself onward, running back down the rubble until he was on flat ground again. Tonight he would circle Enchanted Mesa until the gods told him to stop.

But the pounding of the storm had no mercy and Kendall was soon blinded by rain hitting his face. His legs gave out and he fell facedown, mud oozing up his nose. Once down, Kendall couldn't get back up. He lay there and wondered vaguely if he could sleep on the ground all night. He'd end up drowning before morning.

Something tickled his fingers, and Kendall jerked his hand, thoughts of a rattler sliding over his arm. Then a warm nose nudged his face and Kendall rolled over. Rasmiyah stood white against the black night like a dream. Except that she wasn't a dream. She was real. She snorted and whinnied in her throat, licking his hand and then nibbling his face. Kendall laughed with relief and joy. She had found him.

"I can't get up," he told her.

She bent her head and poked him once more, stamping her hooves impatiently against the muddy earth. When he didn't move, she pranced around in a circle, shaking her wet, tangled mane.

Kendall fought the urge to lay there forever and slowly sat up. It took all his strength to stand again. Rasmiyah didn't bolt or shy away.

He reached out a hand to her and the white horse came close, pushing up against Kendall's body. He just stood there, not understanding. Then she nipped him on the shoulder and pushed her neck into his, almost knocking him over.

Rain and tears mixed together, salt and dirt running into his mouth as Kendall wrapped his arms around her neck. He ran his hands down her back and then reached up to stroke her forelock. Grumbling in her throat, the mare trotted off a few paces, then returned to Kendall's side. The run would be his last one for the summer. And this time Rasmiyah was going to run with him.

Rain stung Kendall's bare back as they galloped into the night. The magic power of the gods reeled him in, his legs moving in time with Rasmiyah. Lightning splintered the sky, illuminating the cactus and the silhouette of Enchanted Mesa. Kendall felt as if he were sliding in and out of sleep as he ran.

When they had nearly circled Enchanted Mesa, Kendall

snapped back to consciousness when someone from the darkness called out his name.

"Kendall," the voice summoned, as though it came from the very mountain itself. He stared through the grim midnight rain.

No sign of anyone. Prickles ran down his spine.

"Kendall," it murmured again. Soft, yet distinct. Instantly he recognized the voice, but how could that be?

Then he heard something he hadn't heard for a long time. A name only his mother knew. His Acoma name. The name he hadn't heard since she died. Even Rasmiyah halted as if she heard the voice, too.

With trembling hands, Kendall dug into his pouch and pulled out the dream catcher, holding it up. Strands of magic seemed to pull through the weaving as it hovered in the air before him. And she was there inside the magic, her long black hair streaming like raindrops behind her.

The memories came flooding back, and Kendall knew he would always remember one of the last things she told him. "Whenever you run, Kendall, run with everything inside your heart."

Enchanted Mesa's silence had broken. He had followed the magic over the demanding path it required, and tonight Kendall had earned a vision from the gods. But the gods didn't have to tell him who he was. Instead, his running had told the gods who he was, and Kendall felt the mantle of his great-grandfather's Snake power fall on his shoulders.

Beyond the darkness lay the miniature twin of Enchanted Mesa, with magical cords stronger than Kendall could endure. The secrets of the ancient Snake Clan lay here in this land. He was the last of the clan, but without knowledge of the past or the source of the magic.

The last person to know was gone. Kendall had barely begun to find his legacy. Was it too late? He'd skimmed the surface of something deep and powerful. Answers were buried deep in the magic. Sometime in the future Kendall knew they would lead him back to those roots.

The magic filled his legs and arms, and Kendall began to run again, slowly retracing his steps across the valley floor. Rasmiyah followed beside him, her breath warm on his face. The sudden sound of footsteps came up behind him and Kendall turned to look over his shoulder.

A shadowy figure, naked except for deerskin apron, ran on bare, silent feet. Black hair, no longer white, fell to the runner's waist, fluttering in an unseen breeze as he ran past Kendall and disappeared into the enveloping night.

A moment later, the wild herd of horses appeared out of the rain and mist. Rasmiyah nudged Kendall's shoulder, then lifted her front legs and darted off into the night, following the other mares and stallions.

Kendall forced himself not to run after them toward the magic. It was harder than he thought, and for a moment he stood, torn between two places. Then he turned and reached for the shimmering waves of enchantment in the opposite direction.

Through the storm, a set of headlights glared like two white beacons on the road sweeping past Enchanted Mesa, several hundred yards to the north. The truck's lights didn't move on the empty stretch of narrow pavement, but shone patiently, waiting for him. As Kendall ran closer, he could hear the engine's familiar noisy rumble as it idled in the rain.

When he reached the truck, the passenger door swung open. Dad pulled him inside and hugged him fiercely. The truck's seats, Dad's shirt, and the half-open maps strewn about the cab were instantly soaked.

Kendall glanced at Brett, who sat hunched over the steering wheel, staring at him.

"You're looking pretty good, runner boy," his brother told him, grinning.

"Let's go," Dad said thickly.

Brett ground the gears and slowly made a U-turn.

Leaning forward, Kendall put his arms up on the dash and stared through the windshield. The wipers worked at full speed across the glass as more rain pounded like rocks against the metal roof of the truck. Then a flash of lightning lit up the desert, illuminating Enchanted Mesa for the last time. In that split second, Kendall saw that the desert was empty. The horses were gone. Any spirits of past Snake runners were also gone—forever. But part of Kendall ran with them, would always run with them. He was an Acoma runner of the Snake Clan. And he would be back.

Taking his hands off the dash, Kendall leaned deep into his dad's side and let the magic take him home.

AUTHOR'S NOTE

Although Kendall and his family are fictional characters, the exquisite pueblo of Acoma in New Mexico, the Land of Enchantment, does exist. The history and depictions in this story are based on Acoma's own oral and recorded tribal history, as well as written records by Spanish explorers and modern-day historians.

The last known date of the Snake Dances at Acoma are only briefly hinted at in a record by Antonio de Espejo, a Spanish explorer, traveling through the Southwest in 1582. No one knows the details of the ceremonies or exactly when the Snake Clan stopped performing them, but most likely they were similar to the Snake Ceremonies of the Hopi and other Pueblo tribes of the Southwest.

At the beginning of the seventeenth century the population of the Snake Clan at Acoma began to shrink. The last living member of the Snake Clan, an elderly man, died in the 1920s, taking any history or knowledge with him to the grave.

Is there magic at Acoma? That depends entirely on your point of view. I have visited this haunting desert land and the village of Sky City on top of the mesa numerous times. It seems as though powerful spirits from the past dwell alongside the present. I could swear, at times, that one can fleetingly glimpse a girl from hundreds of years ago carrying a tinaja jar on her head as she descends the steep rock paths to the water cisterns.

Because I have felt the magic of Acoma—Kendall's magic—I wanted to write about it, and I carry it with me whenever I am away from Acoma.